<u>Mac Ireland</u>

The Cause Endures

Published by Mac Ireland Publications

P.O. Box 15128

Washington, D.C. 20003-0849

SeanMcManus6@mac.com

ISBN-13: 978-1508813606

ISBN-10: 1508813604

CreateSpace, North Charleston, SC

Cover design: Barbara J. Flaherty

Dramatis Personae

Characters in the Book

BOOK ONE

Brady, Roger	Patriotic helper
Brogan, Harry	Chief of staff of IRA
Cassidy Brothers	(Jack and Peter) New York cops
Duffy, Lizzie	Great Aunt of Mick Duffy
Duffy, Mick	Secret associate
Flynn, Michael	Special Branch, British Agent
Fratelli, Vincent	IRA Internal Security, British Agent
Gaffney, Chris	Quartermaster of Belfast IRA
Johnson, Bobbie	Sammy Johnson's cousin
Johnson, Sammy	Protestant detective
Johnson, Vera	Sammy Johnson's aunt
Jones, Benny	Local IRA volunteer
Kelly, Brian	Top Special Branch man
Mac Ireland, Patrick	Legendary IRA Hero
Mac Ireland, Ultan	Patrick's brother
Maguire, Father Fergal	Parish priest in Kincally
Mc Caffrey, Hugh	NY Cop, former IRA man
Mc Cormac, Mickey	Contact man for Mac Ireland
Mc Donough, Mary	Patrick Mac Ireland's wife
Mc Govern, Jimmy	Replacement for Packie Murray
Mc Nally, Eammon	Second in command of local IRA
Moore, Robert	SAS member
Mulligan, Emmet	IRA leader, British Agent
Murphy, Terrence, Fr.	Priest in Washington, D.C.

Murray, Packie	Local IRA man
O'Connell, Sean	New Chief of Staff of IRA
O'Neill, Kevin	Second in command to Mac Ireland
O'Neill, Liam	Kevin's brother and replacement
Reilly, Seamus	Trusted messenger
Richardson, Emily	American reporter
Shepherd, Charlie	SAS assassin
Sheridan, Pedar	Mac Ireland's driver

BOOK 2

Devonworth, Henry George	MI5, Second in Command
Donegan, Paddy	Special Branch man
Fitzgarret, Gerald	TD, British Agent
Hatcher, Margaret	British Cabinet Minister
Heath, Hamilton Sydney	Director of Special Forces
Mossie Meany	Dubliner, IRA supporter
O'Brien, Connie	TD, British Agent
O'Lynch, Seamus	TD, British Agent
O'Malley, Dessie	Special Branch man
Small, James	British Intelligence Coordinator

BOOK 3

Brassington-Breckenridge, II, Edward J.	Director of Special Forces
Chapman, Harry	SAS Group Leader
Collins, Mick	Redemptorist Brother
Gorev, Boris	Soviet Diplomat
Kowalski, Father Jakub	Pope John Paul's confidant
Mc Corry, Jeffey	CIA Agent
Smith, Freddie	Intelligence Liaison

EPIGRAPH

"Yea, from the table of my memory

I'll wipe away all trivial fond records,

All saws of books, all forms, all pressures past,

That youth and observation copied there;

And thy commandment all alone shall live

Within the book and volume of my brain,

Unmixt with baser matter; yes, by heaven!"

Hamlet. Act 1. Scene V. 98-104

CHAPTER I

(End of August 1980)

Patrick Mac Ireland—the most wanted IRA leader in Ireland, North or South—was listening to the Irish news in his bolt-hole in France. Well, actually, he was listening to his wife, Mary Mc Donough, read out her translations of the French newspapers. Mary was, along with her many other gifts, a fluent French speaker and writer—not to mention an expert in the Irish language.

Mary was reading aloud about Mac Ireland's latest exploits: the death of two Irish politicians who had been found dead floating off the coast of West Cork—one of the most southern parts of the island of Ireland.

With her gently tinged County Cavan accent, Mary translated. "'Time of death has not been determined. Foul play may be suspected, but the Irish police are being reticent.' Another newspaper, which had sent a French journalist to West Cork, reported the local reaction. 'Ah, God bless us all; it's terrible...May they rest in peace.' But others weighed in very strongly. 'Look, I don't welcome the death of any man, but it also must be said that those two, O'Lynch and O'Brien, were the two worst Irishmen since John Redmond.' 'Excuse me,' another man interjected. 'Redmond wasn't that bad after all, but I agree those two were useless.' According to the reporter, one young man about eighteen, who did not want to be identified, declared, 'I don't know if the IRA killed those two bastards or not. But if they were traitors, then they deserved to be shot, for who else in this bloody country would bring them to justice?'"

Mary kept translating aloud. "An elderly, educated man in Baltimore expressed it this way: 'If two Englishmen sold out their country, as O'Lynch and O'Brien have sold out ours, the Brits would have them shot immediately. If two Americans sold out the United States, the CIA would hunt them down to the ends of the earth. If two Israelis sold out the State of Israel, the Mossad would follow them to the gates of hell, and there would not be a word about it. Every man, apparently, can fight for his country, but if an Irishman were to fight for his country, then it becomes a huge, huge issue. That double standard drives me crazy. And it's what drives young people to take desperate action…I am not saying I support the IRA, but I am saying the real fundamental problem in this partitioned country will never be addressed if the Dublin government doesn't have the guts to stand up to England. Our cowardly, gutless politicians are an absolute (excuse the language) fucking disgrace.'" Mary paused before she started on another newspaper, looking over at Mac Ireland.

"Check, Mary, if there is anything about our bringing to justice the two hanged men," he asked.

Mary rapidly turned the pages as she scanned the news. "Oh, yes, here it is. 'Two men were found mysteriously hanged in a country hay shed near The Border with the Irish Republic. Foul play is suspected. The bodies of a well-known Belfast IRA man and a top British intelligence officer were discovered when neighbors entered a Protestant farmyard in the parish of Kincally, County Fermanagh.'"

Then without prompting from Mac Ireland, Mary translated about the gun battle Mac Ireland and his Number Two, Liam O'Neill, had had with six members of the SAS, all of whom were killed.

Mary then sat down, finished with the reading and the translations from French.

"Patrick, it's another miracle the Brits did not get you and Liam—or Sammy Johnson, the brave Protestant detective from the North who is taking so many risks with you," she said.

"I know, Mary, I know, and while you're at it, don't forget Mick Duffy. As a Free State Special Branch man, Mick is taking huge risks," said Mac Ireland.

Mary sighed and wondered. "If it were not so scary, it would be so ironic—Sammy, from a respected Fermanagh Protestant and Unionist family with a long tradition of serving the British Army, and RUC, working with you, the most famous IRA man in the country! And then Mick Duffy—because he was so disgusted by the sell-out of the Dublin government—joins forces with you and with Sammy, and helps you to execute British Agents and Special Branch men who have become British Agents...I mean, Patrick, who would believe it. I understand it is your duty, but I am really frightened...And then Liam O'Neill, whom I love like a brother-in-law, poor, brave Liam—your closest colleague of all—he, too, is in enormous danger...I feel we are so alone..."

Mac Ireland sat silently, absorbing Mary's words and feelings—helping her "to carry her cross," as his mother would have put it. This segued him into thinking of the poem Patrick Pearse wrote for his own mother:

The Mother
By Pádraig Pearse (1916)

I do not grudge them: Lord, I do not grudge
My two strong sons that I have seen go out
To break their strength and die, they and a few,
In bloody protest for a glorious thing,
They shall be spoken of among their people,
The generations shall remember them,
And call them blessed;
But I will speak their names to my own heart
In the long nights;
The little names that were familiar once
Round my dead hearth.
Lord, thou art hard on mothers:
We suffer in their coming and their going;
And tho' I grudge them not, I weary, weary
Of the long sorrow—And yet I have my joy:
My sons were faithful, and they fought.

Mary, looking at him intently, understood that he shared her feeling and knew her fears. She knew he feared that she would be assassinated to penalize him, that even though nobody—except a trusted few—knew they were married, the risks were still dangerously high. But she was prepared to take those risks because she loved him totally. She had told him over and over again, "Go and free Ireland, and I will take care of everything else."

Mary loved rubbing it into him that they were rich, knowing he felt uncomfortable about money. "I am rich," she would say, teasing him, "so get over it. That means you are rich too...For richer or poorer, remember!"

For the time and circumstances—County Cavan, in the 1970s—Mary was, indeed, rich. Her grandfather had left her a fortune, and just recently her granduncle in America had left her a bequest of $30 million. "You mind our poor oppressed country, Patrick, and I will mind ***our*** money," she adored telling him.

Mac Ireland, however, for all his disquiet about riches, was greatly relieved that he did not have to worry about financially supporting Mary while he was "on the run." Having to fight for Irish freedom, while neglecting one's family, would be a horrendous position to be in. Yet many IRA Volunteers all over Ireland were in that position, and he was most sensitive to it.

Despite the danger of it all, Mac Ireland felt blessed. Fighting for Irish justice gave him peace of mind—that unique peace of mind that only results from following one's conscience. Like any patriot the world over, Mac Ireland knew he would never have peace of mind if he turned his back on his country and left the fighting to women and children in Belfast, while their husbands and fathers were in British prisons in The North.

Above all, Mac Ireland felt blessed because of his extraordinary wife—the beautiful, smart, and courageous Cavan lassie. Now the Cavan lassie was trying to get his focus, calling his name several times. When that failed, she playfully tossed a tiny teddy bear on his lap. "Hey, Boy from the Erne, come back to me."

He smiled. "I hadn't gone away from you. I was closer to you than you can imagine, sweetheart."

Mary shot back, "Now you are being sweet to me just

because I'm rich." She doubled up in laughter. Mac Ireland did his involuntary wince and then chuckled at her merriment.

Suddenly the phone rang; Mary jumped up and answered it. "It's Fr. Murphy in Washington," she shouted.

CHAPTER 2
May 1981

In the month since Fr. Murphy's telephone call, Patrick Mac Ireland lay very low, only slipping into Ireland a few times to arrange large consignments of weapons from the continent. The Irish Hunger Strike was beginning to reach its peak, with Bobby Sands—leader of the ten hunger strikers—fast approaching death.

No leading IRA man could easily move around given the massive security. Also, Mac Ireland did not want to take any action that would distract from or overshadow the extraordinary sacrifice of the ten brave Irish patriots. However, Mac Ireland, as always, stayed busy.

Mac Ireland could not get out of his head the most unusual nature of Fr. Murphy's telephone call: Did Mac Ireland know anyone with Soviet connections? Yes, anyone who would have connections with the Politburo—the Central Committee of the Communist Party of the Soviet Union—headed by Leonid Brezhnev since 1964 to the present day.

Mac Ireland had responded—on a phone line both he and Fr. Murphy knew was absolutely safe, "Now, Fr. Terence, I know you don't believe the Brit lie that the Movement is Communist-connected, so what is this all about?"

"I cannot go into to it on the phone, but you know the

place where people, like you, take their religion from, but not their politics. Well, there is concern that the Communists have penetrated the administration...and I've been asked to help. I will come and see you in France on Sunday, May 17."

Before hanging up, Fr. Murphy said, "I am very sorry about Bobby Sands. It is now May 2; he cannot last much longer. Did you ever know him?"

"No, I never did, but I know the second hunger striker in line: Francis Hughes. He is one of the best we've ever had—a fearless, intrepid fighter."

After Fr. Murphy hung up, Mac Ireland was in a total quandary. He, of course, naturally picked up on Fr. Murphy's code words, "the place where people, like you, take their religion from, but not their politics." The "place" was clearly Rome, referring to the famous mantra of Irish republicanism, "We take our religion from Rome, but our politics from home." Rome meaning the Vatican. So what the heck was this business about Communist penetration? He let his mind wander freely.

Mac Ireland knew that in certain extreme pockets of Catholicism, some believed that Pope John XXIII's Second Vatican Council (1962–1965) was a Communist plot—it had approved Mass being said in the vernacular, not in compulsory Latin. He was also aware that that change had disturbed many ordinary, moderate Catholics. One of the reassuring signs for Catholics of that time was that Mass had been said in Latin since AD 399—a powerful example of oneness, tradition, and universality of the Catholic Church. Furthermore, Mac Ireland knew, one of the reasons was that, since Latin was a "dead" language (no longer spoken in any country), the clear, reliable meaning of its words would never change. Therefore, the teaching of Jesus Christ about the Eucharist would be safeguarded and preserved, and the faith of Catholics all over the world would be uniform, not shattered into a million pieces like the Protestant denominations that emerged from the Reformation in 1517.

In a way—Mac Ireland was aware from his extensive reading—the Church's position on the Latin Mass had been like its desire to preserve the Bible—especially the New Testament, the canon of which the Catholic Church had decided on. Preserving the integrity and accuracy of the Bible had always been the Church's top concern.

St. Augustine (354–430) had complained of the "infinite variety of Latin translations." Therefore, Pope Damasus I in AD 382 commissioned St. Jerome to produce a standard Latin Bible that would be accurate and readable for the common man. It became known as the Vulgate, from the phrase "version vulgate": the common version.

How ironic, Mac Ireland, often thought, that the Catholic Church would be later accused of trying to keep the Bible from the people when it was the Church that produced the "common" (popular) version of the Bible. Not only that, it was the Roman Catholic Church (the Church of Rome and the Church at Rome) that gave the world the canon of the New Testament and the Christian canon of the Hebrew scriptures (Old Testament) intentionally and deliberately joining two blocks of scriptures, thus producing what is known today as the Bible. This was formalized by the Decree of the Council of Rome (AD 382) on the canon of scripture during the reign of Pope Damasus I (AD 366–384). It was known that such a creation (the scriptures in one volume) existed earlier. The famed theologian Tertullian in his *Prescription against Heretics* (AD 200) praised the steadfastness of the Church of Rome, which had "united in one volume" the scriptures "from which she drinks in her faith."

However, as often happens in history, the "means" (in this case, the Latin language) almost became the "end"—preserving Latin became synonymous with preserving the accuracy of the Bible. The Catholic Church—out of fear the exact and proper meaning of the Bible would be lost in translation—opposed *unauthorized* translations of the Bible into English. Not that those fears were completely unfounded. For instance, in 1380—the year John Wycliffe (1330–1384) initiated the translation of the complete English Bible (partial translations had been made much earlier)—there was still no Standard English language.

England had almost as many local dialects as it had shires (counties). People from different counties had difficulty understanding each other, often thinking that the others were speaking French. After all, it was only as recent as 1363 that the British Parliament had opened for the first time with an English speech. Previously, French had been the language of the court. Therefore, the fear of the Catholic Church, which had preserved the Bible, was not entirely unfounded. Additionally, the Catholic Church had to be forever mindful of St. Peter's warning, "No prophecy of Scriptures is a matter of private interpretation" (2 Pet. 1:20); and "some difficult passages [in St. Paul], the meaning of which the ignorant and untrained distort, as they do also in the case of other Scriptures, to their own ruin" (2 Pet. 3:16). Add to all that, when renegade priests—like Wycliffe and William Tyndale (1494–

1536), who may have been admirable men, but inevitably renegade in the eyes of the Church of that time—accompanied their translations with anti-Catholic screeds and rants, it is not surprising that things fell apart.

Even St. Thomas More—now regarded as the judicious guardian of truth and tradition, even by American Fundamentalists—believed that "any good Christian man having any drop of wit in his head" had to oppose Tyndale's translations. Going further, and away over the top, More declared that searching for errors in the Tyndale New Testament was "like searching for water in the sea."

King Henry VIII—that devout paragon of Catholic virtue—also opposed Tyndale and had his translations banned and burned—until he decided to found the Church of England so he could divorce his wife and marry Anne Boleyn. Tyndale, for all his opposition to the pope's overweening power, had conveniently preached the Divine Right of Kings. "He that judgeth the King, judgeth God and damneth God's law and ordinance...The King is, in this world, without law: and may at his lust do right or wrong, and shall give account to God alone." Right up Henry's alley.

However, it must be acknowledged that Tyndale's translations would go on to significantly shape and influence the incomparable King James Bible of 1611. Still, it equally has to be acknowledged that the said King James I had also commanded his forty-seven gifted scholar-editors to make sure that their translations conformed to the theology and tradition of the Anglican Church—then in existence since 1534, a mighty total of seventy-seven years! So, Mac Ireland always groused, seventy-seven years of Anglican "tradition" trumped 1,534 years of

Catholic tradition, which had established and preserved the canon of the New Testament and had given the Bible to the world.

Nonetheless, the English Bible was of historic importance. It made a huge contribution to the development of the English language, enabling the English people to become the most literate in Europe, and empowered ordinary people to think for themselves. Well, to think for themselves, at least in theory. English Protestants had relied on the power of the monarchy to break the power of the pope, but ended up ceding all spiritual power to the monarch. Denying spiritual power to the Vicar of Christ on Earth (the pope) and entirely investing it in kings and queens was of questionable spiritual validity, and it made a mockery of apostolic succession. (Apostolic succession is the unbroken line of bishops—and, of course, of popes—that goes back to the time of the apostles. All Catholic bishops are part of that lineage, which is not, therefore, possible in the Protestant churches—most of which do not even claim to have bishops, anyway.) Although some popes had been of dubious spirituality, at least the papacy could make a better claim to represent the One, Holy, Catholic, and Apostolic Church.

For example, King James I—he of the King James Bible—could claim that a king was "God's lieutenant... and could frame his actions according to law, yet he was not bound thereto, but above all restraints except his own inspired will." How convenient!

Nearly all the Catholic bishops in England went belly-up, rejected the Vicar of Christ, and embraced kings and queens as heads of the Church. The original sin of the Anglican Church made possible by the collusion of

Catholic bishops!

It is often grandly asserted that the Reformation was the mother of modern democracy. But democracy for whom? Certainly not the Irish. The Reformation unleashed centuries of increased brutal oppression. The English Bible was used as the prime justification for that oppression. Queen Elizabeth and Cromwell could posture as English Joshuas, divinely mandated to slay without mercy the indigenous people—the "Canaanite" Irish. That should surely has meant that henceforth the Irish all over the world should have learned to read the Bible through the eyes of the Canaanites. As Arnold Toynbee, the doyen of British historians, says, it was the "biblically recorded conviction of the Israelites that God had instigated them to exterminate the Canaanites" that sanctioned British oppression and genocide in Ireland.

What sort of a daughter was Elizabeth (1533–1603) to her mother, Anne Boleyn? What daughter could ignore the fact that her father (King Henry VIII) had murdered her mother—chopping off her head on the false charges of adultery, incest, and high treason? If Elizabeth had any honor or daughterly love for her slaughtered mother, she should have rejected, root and branch, the system—the "reformed" church and state—that triggered such savagery. Instead, she accepted the Crown, ensuring that corruption would continue to be passed down in a hereditary monarchy. Moreover, she, Her Royal Self, would indulge in the ethnic cleansing of Ireland—expelling and dispossessing the native Irish, replacing them with English and Scottish Protestants. "Good Queen Bess"! Yeah, tell that to Mary Queen of Scots, whose head Good Queen Bess chopped off.

What sort of a son was King James 1 (1566–1625) to his mother, Mary Queen of Scots? How could he calmly accept his mother's head being cut off by Queen Elizabeth, and then succeed Elizabeth to the English throne?

King James—whom Protestants would almost want to canonize because of his Bible—justified his strange relation (especially for that time) with George Villiers in these immortal words: "I wish to speak in my own behalf and not to have it thought to be a defect, for Jesus Christ did the same, and therefore I cannot be blamed. Christ had his John, and I have my George." He is an ironic hero, indeed, for Northern Ireland and American fundamentalist Protestants.

Then the Reformation cursed the Irish with Oliver Cromwell (1599–1658), war criminal and murderous maniac—the Taliban of his time, and the hero of all anti-Catholic bigots. Now the Irish are told they should admire that historical era, appreciating it as the flowering of democracy, freedom of conscience, and religious liberty. What a joke!

What sort of a daughter was Mary (1662–1694) to King James II? She was married to her first cousin William III of Orange (1650–1702). English Protestants treasonously conspired against King James II, and invited William to come from Holland and usurp the Crown. Mary went along with the high treason, and she and William became Queen and King of England. That led to the anti-Catholic section of The Act of Settlement, 1701—still in force today—which prohibits the monarch from being a Catholic. This constitutionally enshrined bigotry fundamentally guarantees the allegiance of the Orange Order and the Protestants/Unionists of the North of Ireland, while providing the moral underpinnings of anti-Catholic discrimination in the North. If Catholics by law cannot get the top job (king or queen), they are by definition inferior, and it is proper to discriminate against them. Indeed— the perverse logic reasons—one proves he is a loyal Protestant by treating Catholics as second-class citizens.

To show there was also continuity of tradition in the inbred Royal Family, King Billy—as the Orangemen love to call him—had as his mistress George Villiers's relative Elizabeth Villiers. King James I "had his George," and King Billy "had his Elizabeth."

That period, if one can believe it, was called the Glorious Revolution. Yet it ushered in an escalated reign of anti-Catholic rule and oppression that lasted right up to 1920 in all of Ireland, and after that date in Northern Ireland.

Not surprisingly, the suffering and oppressed Irish were not too enamored of this newly invented religion. The famous blind poet Raftery (1784–1835) captured the common Irish cynicism and resentment thus:

Don't talk of your Protestant Minister
Or his church without Temple or state
For the foundation of his religion
Was the bollocks of Henry VIII.

It was hard for the Irish to be ecumenical toward the new religion when it was dedicated to the destruction of the Irish spirit and faith. It was difficult to appreciate the beauty of the King James Bible when it was used to humiliate the Irish and to justify genocide.

***

All that history flashed through Mac Ireland's mind

at the thought of the Latin Mass, even though he himself was delighted that the Mass was now in the vernacular.

He also knew that Fr. Murphy was a moderate and learned man who did not indulge in fantasies or conspiracy theories about the Vatican.

What could Fr. Murphy possibly mean by "Communist penetration," and what did it have to do with the IRA or himself? Mac Ireland remained perplexed by it all.

***

Meanwhile, on May 5, poor Bobby Sands heroically died after sixty-six days on hunger strike, sowing more dragon's teeth for the Brits. Then on May 12, the gallant Francis Hughes died after fifty-nine days on hunger strike.

It broke Mac Ireland's heart because he feared the remaining eight hunger strikers would also die under the racist, anti-Irish, and anti-Catholic British government.

"Absolutely, more dragon's teeth," Mac Ireland could imagine his number two, Liam O'Neill, promising. Mac Ireland reflected how he had not so long ago explained to O'Neill the reference to Cadmus, in Greek mythology, who slew the dragon and sowed its teeth: "When they were sown, there arose from the ground armed men..."

When Mac Ireland had said it was a wonderful metaphor for what the Brits had done in Ireland, the dedicated young Tyrone freedom fighter replied, "I like that; it fits, it really fits. We are the armed men, and the Brits and their collaborators will reap what they sowed."

Thinking of O'Neill naturally led Mac Ireland to think of his other two colleagues: Sammy Johnson and Mick Duffy.

Johnson was the Protestant detective from Belfast whose son and aunt had been murdered by British Agents.

In an extraordinary turn of events—granting the polarized history of Northern Ireland—Johnson had joined Mac Ireland in his campaign to exact justice on the British assassins. To add to the unheard-of nature of the alliance, Mick Duffy, a Special Branch man in the Free State (the twenty-six counties of the Irish Republic) had also become part of Mac Ireland's elite team. Duffy had become disgusted with how the Dublin government had sold out to the British, and had discovered that the Brits had practically taken over the Special Branch and key Southern politicians.

I wonder what Liam, Sammy, and Mick would make of Fr. Murphy's call,

Mac Ireland thought to himself. But he knew he could not tell them, at least not just yet.

CHAPTER 3
May 13, 1981

Mac Ireland was having a nap when his wife Mary burst into the bedroom screaming, "Patrick they shot the pope! They shot the pope!"

Mac Ireland, still sleepy, raised himself on his right elbow and asked, "What pope?"

"Oh, for God's sake, Patrick, how many popes do you think we have?"

Mac Ireland, now fully awake, groaned, "Oh my God, they shot Pope John Paul II?"

"Yes, but he is only wounded, and he's expected to live," explained Mary.

Mac Ireland followed her out to the sitting room, and Mary translated the French news as it came on TV.

"I wonder if that means Fr. Murphy will not come now," Mac Ireland asked Mary.

Before she could answer, the phone rang and she grabbed it. "It's Fr. Murphy," she said as she handed the phone over to Mac Ireland.

"Hello, Father, I was just after saying to Mary that I was wondering if would you still come," said Mac Ireland.

"It's now more important than ever," explained Fr. Murphy. "I'll be there at your place on Sunday afternoon as promised." He hung up.

Now Mac Ireland was back to wondering what it was all about. However, he thought to himself, I am not going over all that stuff again in my head—about the Bible, the Latin Mass, and the Reformation in England. It was not easy for a politically and theologically conscious Irishman to block out the Protestant Reformation as it happened in England and was brutally imposed on Ireland. He was still living with the effects because whereas before the Reformation, Catholic England had viciously oppressed Catholic Ireland, now Protestant England had an extra means of oppression: sectarian anti-Catholicism. Another club to beat down the Irish, and England would recruit the Bible as one of its main justifications. Crushing "heathen" Catholics was God's will. Total domination of Ireland was divinely mandated for the purity of the faith—not, of course, out of greed and colonial plunder but out of sheer altruism and for the sake of God's kingdom on earth.

When England in 1920 created the artificial and undemocratic State of Northern Ireland, good Protestants, now the artificial majority, had to keep "unbiblical" Catholics in their place—just like good white Christians in Mississippi had to keep blacks in their place. Yes, in 1980, Mac Ireland had to live with the pernicious effects of the English Reformation, which had only brought added anti-Catholic sectarianism, heaped upon English racism. He felt that whereas the Reformation in Europe was basically a religious movement, the English Reformation was in large part a political movement.

Mac Ireland had to shake himself to get it all out of his head.

"Let's go for a long walk," he said to Mary. "I need to get into the fresh air and clear my head." Mary gladly agreed, as she loved their long walks.

On Sunday afternoon at noon, Fr. Murphy arrived. Mac Ireland proudly introduced Mary, and all three sat down at the table for tea and biscuits.

When Fr. Murphy had heard all about Mary, he turned to Mac Ireland and said, "Now Patrick, I have to talk to you about something really pressing and important. Needless to say, it is strictly confidential and extremely sensitive. Because it is not strictly IRA business, I think Mary should hear it, too. Indeed, she may be able to help." Both Mac Ireland and Mary nodded their consent.

Fr. Murphy finished his cup of tea, accepted another one from Mary, and said, "I have known a Polish priest, Fr. Jakub Kowalski, in Chicago for more than thirty years. He's originally from Poland and is a close, close friend of Pope John Paul II. They grew up together in Wadowice, Poland. Jakub has been confidentially advising the pope for many years. Indeed, the pope listens to Jakub more than to anyone. Jakub is a top expert on Communism and Soviet rule in Poland, Russia, and East Germany. The Soviets are deeply worried about Pope John Paul. While he was archbishop of Cracow, the SB—Sluzba Bezpieczenstwa, the Polish Secret Police—had him totally bugged. And even though he is now pope, the Soviets are watching his every move because they have their spies in the Vatican—lay and clerical spies."

At the mention of clerical spies, Mary couldn't help gasping. "Clerical spies working for the Communists, in the Vatican, against the pope?"

"I'm afraid so, Mary. I'm afraid so." Fr. Murphy sighed. "Indeed, it is so bad, that the pope cannot trust the Vatican's normal communication systems. Anything related to Communism, and he has to use outside sources."

Mac Ireland groaned. "If the Communists can do that to the Vatican and to Polish clergy, can you imagine what the British intelligence has done in Ireland?" Then turning to Fr. Murphy, Mac Ireland said, "Not meaning to cut you short, Father, but what has this to do with me and the IRA?"

Fr. Murphy put his hands together on the table, almost as if he were at the altar, lowered his head as if in prayer, then staring intently at Mac Ireland asked, "Do you remember telling me some years ago about the Soviet intelligence operator who came to see you in Ireland—the secret Catholic?"

Mac Ireland hadn't thought of that person in years, actually had forgotten about him. Fr. Murphy interjected, "So that Mary will be on the same page, and to refresh my own memory, why don't you tell the story about him."

"Well, okay, let me see if I can reconstruct it," Mac Ireland said. "In 1969, the IRA split into the so-called Officials, who were led by Marxists, and the Provisionals, led by the more traditional Irish Republicans. The Soviets naturally supported—at least nominally and to some degree—the Officials (Stickies).

"I remained friendly with some of the Officials, who were decent enough guys and who weren't using Marxist analysis to avoid fighting the Brits—you know the nonsense about how we cannot fight until the Protestant working class will join us in one united movement and kick England into the sea. Anyway, after the split, a good Stickie contacted me to see if I would meet with a Soviet intelligence operator who was doing an analysis of the Irish situation. I agreed. I met Boris Gorev (if that's his real name) in a hotel in Dublin. He was born and reared in Moscow—a highly intelligent, cultured, and amiable man. He told me he did not think the Stickies would amount to anything. He said that he thought my colleagues and I were the real revolutionaries, and that he would love to support us, but he knew the Soviets would never go along with it because we did not toe the Moscow line.

"Anyway, to make a long story short, we got to know each other very well. I could sense he was a fine man who wanted to confide something to me. After several meetings he did. He confided that his family never had given up the Catholic faith, and that it was the most important thing in his life, and was getting more and more important as every year passed. He was about thirty years old. At that time he was operating out of the Soviet Embassy in Dublin, of course. The last I heard of him he was at the Soviet Embassy in Rome."

"Oh, my goodness, you think he's in Rome?" Fr. Murphy said.

"Okay, now, Father," countered Mac Ireland. "Please, tell me what this is all about. I will answer all sorts of questions, but I really need to know where all this is heading."

"Well to Rome, Patrick, to Rome," said Fr. Murphy. "As they say, all roads lead to Rome. I came to see you because when Fr. Kowalski told me the pope was trying to find a way around the heavy Communist infiltration of the Vatican, I told him about you and your contact with Boris. Fr. Kowalski made some inquiries, and then asked me to go and see you—because approaching the IRA about Vatican business is so improbable, Fr. Kowalski thought it just might work and could be kept secret. I mean, who would ever suspect it? And now—since the attempt on the pope's life—the most urgent thing is to find out who ordered the assassination attempt. Fr. Kowalski does not want to go through normal, official channels because he knows the truth will be buried and covered up. Also, the pope does not want any of this to go public."

"Do you think you can help, Patrick?" said Fr. Murphy. "Let me add that your new big donor in America wants you to help and wants you to use for this project some of the money he is donating."

"Whoa, my goodness, I never saw that coming," said Mac Ireland, and he looked over at Mary.

Mary was clearly in a state of surprise. "This is really amazing," she kept saying to herself. Then she reached out and grasped Mac Ireland's hand, earnestly pleading, "Patrick, if we can help, we have to, we simply must."

"God bless us," said Mac Ireland. "This is a remarkable turn of events."

"We have to. We have to," pressed Mary, adding impishly, "and we've never been to Rome together."

"Aha." Fr. Murphy smiled. "As Patrick likes to say, quoting what St. Thomas Aquinas said, 'there is never a completely altruistic motive.'"

Mary laughed and said, "Come on now, Father, who says one cannot have fun while doing good."

"Have you been to Rome yourself, Mary?" asked Fr. Murphy.

"Oh, several times as a student," replied Mary. "It's almost as wonderful as Cavan. Although not fluent, I can get by speaking the language—I mean in Rome, not Cavan."

"Well, Father, the boss has made your mission easy. She has, it appears, already signed me up." Mac Ireland laughed. Then turning serious again said, "But what are the security implications in all of this for me. As this is emanating from America, I would be concerned that the CIA might know about it, and if they do, then the Brits will know about it."

"The CIA would not be your enemy here," stated Fr. Murphy. Mac Ireland looked at him intently. Fr. Murphy continued, "You know, President Reagan has a great respect for Pope John Paul. He sees him as the single-most important ally against Communism, believing, indeed, that the pope can bring Communism down for all time. I am told that President Reagan intends to send the pope all copies of his correspondence with the Soviets, and will have his own 'outside' means of communicating with the pope."

"If we try to help, where do we start?" asked Mac Ireland.

Fr. Murphy didn't hesitate for a moment. "Obviously you have to head to Rome," he said. "I have a place in mind where you and Mary can stay. It's a very large house, near Vatican Square, owned by an order of nuns who will not be in residence for the next six months. It can accommodate six people. It is very secure and private, totally walled off."

That got Mac Ireland's attention because, if needed, he could bring in his team of O'Neill, Johnson, and Duffy. Who knows, if he was going to mess with such sensitive stuff, he might need them. He could now be taking on not just British intelligence but the KGB as well.

"Patrick, are you still with us?" asked Fr. Murphy.

"Oh, sorry, Father, I was just thinking we have a lot of planning to do."

"Now, remember, Patrick, whatever you find out, you must never reveal who ordered the shooting of the pope," cautioned Fr. Murphy.

"Of course, if the pope had said the right thing when he visited Ireland in 1979, it would have been the Brits who would have shot him," Mac Ireland firmly said.

"Well," said Fr. Murphy, laughing, "you can tell Pope John Paul that yourself when you see him."

Mary was relieved when Fr. Murphy just laughed it off because she knew Patrick felt very strongly that the pope had failed to do his duty in Ireland by not condemning the British government for its brutal treatment of Catholics in The North. The pope had only called on the men of violence (code words for the IRA) to stop fighting—without also calling on the British government to stop its institutionalized violence and on the British Army to stop its dirty war.

Fr. Murphy then took his leave. "Mary, enjoy Rome, and, Patrick, I will be in regular touch with details and instructions from Fr. Jakub."

CHAPTER 4

Three hours after Fr. Murphy left, Mac Ireland and his wife started packing for their road trip to Rome.

Mary was in the kitchen and Mac Ireland was upstairs in the bathroom getting his shaving stuff. He went into the spare bedroom, where his luggage was sitting on the bed.

He looked for space to fit his toilette bag into one of his small cases. His Browning HP—single action nine millimeter semiautomatic pistol with its thirteen-round magazine capacity—was taking up too much space, so he slipped it into the waistband at the back of his pants.

As he was about to go into the main bedroom to put his gun in his backpack, he heard a noise downstairs and shouted to Mary. When she didn't respond, he started to go down the stairs to see what was going on. As he rounded the bend in the staircase, where the kitchen was in full view, Mary screamed out his name in warning.

Then he saw a man was standing behind Mary, his left arm around her neck, and a pistol pointing straight at him. He instinctively ducked, but as he did a bullet slammed into his left side. As Mac Ireland went down, Mary suddenly lifted both her feet off the ground, letting herself drop to the floor—breaking her captor's grip and exposing him completely. Mac Ireland didn't miss a beat—one, two, three shots he blasted into the guy—two to the chest, and one to the head as he went down.

Then Mac Ireland himself sat down on the stairs to steady himself. Mary screamed again, but Mac Ireland thought it was just out of fear and not in warning. He opened his eyes, and another guy was coming toward him, gun extended, in for the kill.

Mary screamed again but this time in rage and defiance. The guy went down on his knees, felled by a mighty wallop, delivered by Mary, from one of those wrought iron pans the French so love to cook with.

Mary stepped aside, well out of the way, and Mac Ireland blasted again: one, two, three. Mary ran toward him. "Patrick, Patrick, you've been hit."

"Stop, Mary, we have to make sure there's not another one of them. Check but be careful."

She stopped in her tracks, went and peered out all the windows, and then carefully went outside. There was only a black car with dark windows; she checked the doors that were unlocked. She ran back inside to where Mac Ireland was standing, shirt off, and pressing it to his wound.

"Patrick, Patrick," she sobbed as she removed the blood soaked shirt to examine him.

"Don't be scared by all the blood, Mary. The bullet just grazed me, went right through. I found it lodged in one of the steps on the staircase. Just stop the bleeding, and I will be all right. But we do have to move quickly and get out of here."

Within ten minutes, Mary had thoroughly cleansed the wound, treating it with antiseptic spray. With a needle and surgical thread, she put in seven stitches and expertly bandaged his wound. She had been shown how to do all that by a Cavan surgeon who had told her—half-jokingly, half-seriously—that if she was going to hang out with Mac Ireland, it was a skill that might come in handy.

Mary then told him to swallow a couple of pain-killing pills (non-aspirin, as aspirin thins blood and can promote bleeding) with a pint of water.

The dizziness soon passed, and Mac Ireland was able to focus on the matter at hand.

With Mary's help—and being extra careful not to make his wound bleed again—he soon had the two Brits (SAS assassins, to be sure) loaded into the trunk of their big black car. He had found the car keys in the pocket of the second guy he had killed. He searched both men and removed their IDs and wallets, leaving no documents on them. He searched their car as well, and removed all documentation.

Mary telephoned her rich friends whose house they had been staying in, explained what happened, and told them she and Patrick had to take off. "Don't worry," was their reply. "As agreed, if asked, our answer is that we rent houses to hundreds of people. You stayed there under a made-up name, you paid cash, and we know nothing else. We will send a team of cleaners over to clean up. Have a safe trip."

Soon Mac Ireland, in the assassins' car, was driving behind Mary as she headed to a secluded, deserted part of the countryside. After about thirty minutes, Mary pulled over.

Mac Ireland drove three hundred yards past her, got out of the big black car, and poured five gallons of petrol all over it, inside and out. He prepared a Molotov cocktail—a large milk bottle filled with gasoline/petrol, with a piece of cloth hanging out of it—lit it with his lighter, and hurled it though the opened back window. Then he ran like hell to Mary's car. Mary took off like a shot. As he looked around, Mac Ireland could see the flames ignite. He put his right hand reassuringly on Mary's left arm.

"Steady now, sweetheart. There's going to be a hell of a bang," he said. Mary steered a steady course as a powerful explosion shattered the peace of the French countryside.

"May God rest their souls," proclaimed Mac Ireland. "I curse the government that sent them to kill and to occupy Ireland."

Mac Ireland saw that Mary was a bit shaken up. He offered to do the driving, but she wouldn't hear of it. "You've been shot, Patrick," she said. "You need to rest. I'm a bit shaken up, but I'm okay. In fact, I am amazed I'm so well, but it's because I feel so lucky to be alive. We both could have been killed."

"Well, I certainly would have been killed had it not been for your quick thinking and intrepid action. I am proud of you, Mary, You did very well."

"Well not too bad, I guess, for a simple Cavan lassie," she beamed.

"Let's drive for about five hours and stay overnight some place," Mac Ireland suggested.

Mary nodded, turned on the radio, and slipped in a Wolfe Tone tape. Mac Ireland dozed off to the strains of a "Nation Once Again" and "The Bold Fenian Men."

CHAPTER 5

After about five hours driving, Mary pulled into a small roadside motel.

They had a bite to eat and settled in for the night.

Mary checked Patrick's bandages and was pleased to see things looked good. She changed the bandages, securing them with duct tape, which Mac Ireland always had in his backpack.

As they lay down, they reviewed their rather extraordinary day—well, at least, out of the ordinary for Mary, not so much for Mac Ireland.

"Sweetheart," Mac Ireland said, "are you sure you're okay? Any danger you're suffering from delayed reaction, a delayed shock sort of thing?"

"Strangely enough," Mary replied, "I think I'm fine. Don't worry love."

Mac Ireland was relieved to hear it, and squeezed her hand. "In the morning, I have to call Sammy Johnson in Belfast," he said. "I want to pass on the IDs of the two SAS assassins to see if he can get a lead on them, and also to see if he can get any information on how they tracked me down. Also, I think we may need him in Rome. Indeed, we may need the entire unusual team—Sammy, Liam O'Neill, and Mick Duffy. If the Brits also track me to Rome, I may need the help of all three of them. Furthermore, it's not just the Brits we may have to contend with. There's the possibility that the KGB may get involved."

"Oh, yes, Patrick, bring them in. I would feel much safer if all three of them were with us. Besides, you now have the money to do it."

"Okay, sweetheart, we'll do it," Patrick agreed. "Regarding tomorrow: we're about four hours from Lyon. So it would be nice to check out that historic city. We could stay the night there and the following morning head for Turin, which is about a four-hour drive, and stay two nights there. Then the following morning we head for Rome, which is about a seven-hour drive."

Mac Ireland turned his head to see if Mary agreed, but she was fast asleep. He smiled in delight as it meant she was not suffering unduly from the trials of the day. He began to silently say the Rosary, and before long he too was out cold.

***

The days passed quickly, too quickly for Mary, and before they knew it, they were arriving at their new digs in the Eternal City.

Mary, who had been educated by nuns, was delighted to be staying in a residence owned by nuns. It was not quite a convent but a residence for nuns while in Rome. It was a pretty good residence, too. Three stories tall, totally enclosed within high walls, with barbed wire on top.

"You have the Men Behind the Wire in The North," Mary joked to Patrick. "Here we have the Women Behind the Wire, and the wire here is not to keep people out, but to keep the nuns in." She laughed. Then, all serious again, she said, "I love the nuns. They have done such heroic and excellent work in Ireland and all over the world.

But now the bigoted and sexist media always want to run them down."

Mac Ireland went to check out the premises: four large bedrooms, two bathrooms, a large kitchen, good-sized sitting room with a large selection of books, and a well-equipped laundry room with a washer, a dryer, and plenty of shelves.

Mac Ireland chose the largest and most secure room for Mary and him. It also had its own bathroom, which he hadn't at first spotted. This will be nice privacy for Mary when the other lads arrive, he thought.

Mac Ireland went to check out the kitchen, but Mary had beaten him to it and handed him a note as he walked in.

"Isn't this nice," she said. "It was taped to the fridge door, saying 'Welcome the friends of Fr. Murphy. If you need anything, please call this number.'"

Mac Ireland nodded in appreciation. Then he checked out the well-stocked, large fridge, knowing they wouldn't have to shop for days. Not that that ever stopped Mary from shopping.

"Sit down, Mary. I will make you a cup of tea, and we will have some great Italian salami, tomatoes, cheese, and wonderful Italian bread."

"Thank you, kind sir." Mary bowed in mock courtesy, delighted, however, by how he was always prepared to cook for her.

When they had finished eating, Mac Ireland said, "In the morning let's go for a long walk, go to Mass in St. Peter's, and then have an Italian breakfast—whatever that is—near St. Peter's Square."

"That would be lovely, Patrick," said Mary.

They did the dishes and then retired for the night, making sure everything was tightly locked up.

CHAPTER 6

Mac Ireland spent the next three days with Mary viewing the sights and taking in the glory of Rome—while never taking his eyes off the mission. He was still waiting to hear back from Sammy Johnson regarding the identities of the two SAS assassins he had killed in France. He was expecting Sammy, Mick Duffy, and Liam O'Neill to arrive within a week. Mac Ireland had also arranged with O'Neill for a trunk full of arms to be delivered to his temporary Roman residence. He had the strongest foreboding they would be badly needed.

Now his immediate task was to make a secure connection with Boris Gorev. Mac Ireland asked Mary to call the Soviet Embassy in Rome, to speak in French, and see if Boris would meet. Surprisingly, she was put right through to Boris. She greeted him in both French and Italian, and then threw in a few words of Irish.

"Ah, Irish, Gaelic." He chortled. "Are you Irish?"

"Yes, I am, and I am married to a red-haired Irishman you met in a hotel in Dublin when you wanted an alternative view—a more traditional view—of the Troubles... More green than red, so to speak." She laughed.

"Oh, yes, yes indeed, how is the famed Patrick Mac Ireland?" enthused Boris.

Boris was only too happy to go to the residence for

a chat.

"May I ask you, without appearing too clichéd, should I have some vodka?" inquired Mary.

"No, no, vodka is never a cliché, only a delight, a joy to the heart, and the perfect way for a son of Russia to renew acquaintance with a son of Ireland, pun intended," Boris chuckled.

When Mary hung up the phone, she said, "I'm off to buy vodka for the charming Boris," kissing Mac Ireland as she left.

***

The following day at 5:00 p.m., Boris arrived, or better, alighted, making his entrance with aplomb and panache. Beautifully dressed—almost like a count—in gold jacket, red waistcoat, and trilby hat—swinging a walking stick. With flair and relish, he kissed Mary on both cheeks and then kissed her hand. As he turned to Mac Ireland, Mac Ireland said, "Boris, let me first take that walking stick from you in case it has a poisoned tip."

Boris erupted in gales of laughter. "Very good, very good, my dear Mac Ireland. Let me give you a Russian bear hug."

When tea was served, Mary poured a shot of vodka for Boris. He sipped it and chortled in delight.

"You shouldn't have, but I'm glad you did—the incomparable Kauffman luxury vintage vodka." He sipped it again, as if wanting to make sure he had correctly identified it, breathing deeply through his nose, mouth closed, as he savored the great texture and flavor. Then he knocked it all back, firmly placing the shot glass on the table, as if he had achieved a remarkable accomplishment.

Mary quickly replenished the empty glass, and Boris

repeated the very same ritual. He sipped, expressed delight and gratitude, did the breathing and savoring thing again, and plopped the glass back on the table. When Mary went to refill it, he put his hand over it.

"No thank you, dear Mary. Well, at least not for the moment. But, as they say in the proud parish of Kincally, the night is still young."

Mac Ireland gasped in surprise that Boris knew about his home parish on the Fermanagh-Cavan border. Boris enjoyed Mac Ireland's obvious surprise. He took out a gold fountain pen and a note pad from his left inside pocket, pulled off two small pages, and wrote something on each page, giving one page to Mary and the other page to Mac Ireland.

"My dear friends, please see my last name on the pages—*Gorev*. Please tell me how, with one stroke of a pen, that quintessential Russian name can be turned into a very Irish name." Mac Ireland looked at his paper, nonplussed.

Mary immediately grabbed Boris's pen and quickly made a stroke, proudly displaying the results. "Change the 'v' into 'y,' and you have the proud Irish name of Gorey," she declared triumphantly.

"Oh, my goodness," Mac Ireland confessed. "I would never have seen that."

Boris reached out and clasped Mac Ireland's left forearm. "Well, let's see if you will see this, Patrick. Did you ever know of any Goreys in your area?"

"No, I don't think so."

"Well, maybe you are thinking only of your father's town-land. What about where you mother came from?"

Mac Ireland was in the middle of scanning his memory on his mother's mountain area when the obvious struck him: how the hell does this Russian guy know about my mother's home area—and, whoa, yes, there were Goreys who lived there at one time. What the heck?

As Mac Ireland found himself tightening up—as his well-honed sense of danger kicked in—he looked challengingly at Boris but eased off as he saw Boris was smilingly understandably, almost tenderly.

"Yes, Patrick, I'm your mother's long-lost neighbor. *I am a Gorey*, across the mountain from your mother's family. My grandfather was Maurice Gorey—not 'Maureece,' as the Americans tend to pronounce it, thinking it is French, but 'Morris,' as the Irish pronounce it."

"My goodness, this is extraordinary," declared Mac Ireland. "I just cannot get away from Kincally!"

"Ah, yes." Boris beamed. "'You can take the Kincally man out of Kincally, but you can't take Kincally out of the Kincally man,' I used to hear my late father say, he having heard it from his father, Maurice."

"Isn't this just lovely," gushed Mary. "Maurice—" Mary smiled sweetly "—I assume is also your real first name—your grandfather changed Gorey to Gorev and Maurice to Boris."

Boris nodded vigorously, all smiles.

"Well, then, Maurice," Mary continued, "this grand homecoming calls for another Kauffman vodka."

"Well, if I were ever going to break my pledge and have a drink, this would be it, but I won't," said Mac Ireland.

"That's right, Patrick, save it until Ireland is free—from the center to the sea, from the sod to the sky," declaimed Boris, proudly displaying his knowledge of the age-old expressions for Irish freedom.

Is there anything this man does not know, wondered Mac Ireland. "Now, Boris," commanded Mac Ireland, "tell us all about Maurice Gorey and what happened after he left the mountain."

Boris, now positively glowing with excitement and with a gentle vodka buzz, began, saying, "My grandfather Maurice was born in 1897, six years before your own mother was born.

Mac Ireland thought, how the heck does he know this, but decided against asking, not wanting to disrupt the flow of the story.

"Maurice left the mountain when he was fifteen years old," said Boris. "He needed to find a job, and there was simply nothing available except joining the British Army, and in principle, his Fenian soul would not permit that, even though, as you know, many future IRA men did join the British Army in those days. Also, it must be said, that he may not have been accepted into the British Army as he was quite frail, with poor eyesight.

"Maurice set out for Liverpool and got onto the first ship—a cargo boat of some type—he could find that was headed for St. Petersburg. For some unknown reason, he was fascinated with Russia. He had 'confiscated' from the Liverpool library a number of books on Russian history and language. It is said that after weeks at sea, he arrived in Russia having taught himself a basic knowledge of the language.

"He moved to Moscow, worked at all sorts of jobs, studied fanatically, and within a few years passed the civil service exams. He was clearly exceptionally intelligent, even though as a growing boy, he had little education, as you can imagine. Anyway, to cut a long story short (as we Kincally men say), within a few years, Maurice was fully embedded in Moscow city management, mostly to do with building codes and infrastructures—a real desk job, which gave him even more time to study.

"He changed his name to Boris Gorev because it was the nearest reconfiguration to his own name that he could come up with. He became completely assimilated into Russian society, and because of his fairly anonymous type of job, he was relatively untouched by the momentous convulsions in the world and the country—World War I and the Russian Revolution. He arrived in Russia in 1912, and seven years later—at only twenty-two years old—Maurice/Boris was a successful and respected man. He had made a fair bit of money in real estate and married my grandmother, Alina, whose family was well off. Alina was a professor of Russian literature."

Boris paused, and being very much the welcome guest, felt free to lift his glass and indicate to Mary that a refill would not be refused. She willingly obliged.

"This is one of the most fascinating things I've ever heard," she told Boris.

Boris grinned in pleasure. "Although Grandfather Maurice/Boris changed in many ways, went all Russian, he never changed in one way. He never gave up his Catholic faith. Indeed, it only got stronger the older he got. When the Communists came to power, he remained steadfastly Catholic.

"He told my father, 'Believe any political or economic theory you want, but never believe the folly that there is no God. Without God nothing works. Without God, man does not make sense.' He firmly believed in the maxim of Dostoevsky, 'If there is no God, everything is permitted'—murder, genocide, endless wars, empires, mass expulsions, and the permanent exploitation of peoples. Just look at the Soviet Empire. How it saddens me to see Russia just mimic the British Empire. But at least Russia is not using the Bible to construct its evil empire."

Both Mary and Mac Ireland were stunned by the honesty and forcefulness of Boris's words.

"Boris, religious-wise, what are you?" asked Mary.

Boris stood up, emptied his vodka, and with great relish pronounced, "I am an Orthodox Irish Catholic!"

Mac Ireland then also stood up, shook Boris hand, and said, "Good for you, Boris. I never believed there were unbridgeable differences between the two Churches—the thousand-year split should never have happened. We both agree on the Blessed Trinity (with different attempted explanations, however) and both agree on the Incarnation, ever mindful that without Mary there would be no Incarnation and, therefore no Redemption."

Boris shyly indicated to Mary to refill his glass, and then astonished her and Mac Ireland by bursting into a magnificent, almost professional rendition of "Amazing Grace" in a perfectly pitched tenor voice, with impeccable enunciation:

Amazing Grace, how sweet the sound,
That saved a wretch like me.
I once was lost but now am found,
Was blind, but now I see.
T'was Grace that taught my heart to fear.
And Grace, my fears relieved.
How precious did that Grace appear
The hour I first believed.

Through many dangers, toils and snares
I have already come;
'Tis Grace that brought me safe thus far
and Grace will lead me home.

Mary, with eyes glistening, rushed over and hugged this extraordinary man, while Mac Ireland clapped heartedly, trying to hide that he too was beginning to get teary-eyed.

"Whoa, guys, this is getting way too powerful," said Mac Ireland. "We need to take a break. Boris, you go and freshen up, the bathroom is down the corridor, and Mary and I will prepare the food. We have some excellent bread, cheese, salami, and all sorts of good stuff. After we eat we can take up where we left off."

"Wonderful, wonderful, I am having one of the most delightful times of my life," Boris said as he headed off to the bathroom.

CHAPTER 7

After a good meal, Boris calmed down somewhat. It had clearly been an emotional few hours for him, with the vodka only playing a minor part in his Irish-Russian excitement and exuberance. It was a point he wanted clearly established.

"Dear friends, Patrick and Mary, please understand it is my Irish heart revealing itself in joy, not the effects of the vodka."

Mac Ireland and Mary nodded in reassurance.

Boris continued, "It is my Russian heart that is speaking when I express alarm over Mother Russia. I am a patriot who loves Russia. I don't want Russia to be an evil empire like the British Empire. I want the Berlin Wall to come down, and I want all people to enjoy national self-determination, independence, and unity. I want to be on the right side of history. It kills my Irish soul to think I am complicit in oppression."

"I totally understand," assured Mac Ireland. "I too am a patriot, and that means for me that I have to take on London, Dublin, and the regime in The North. I know you are a diplomat, so obviously you cannot respond the way I do." Then, making it clear he was changing the thrust of the conversation, Mac Ireland said he wanted to explain why he wanted to meet with Boris.

"Oh, forgive me, forgive me," pleaded Boris. "I got so caught up in the moment I completely forgot."

Mac Ireland nodded that it was okay and said, "This is a delicate issue for both of us. Some of the things you have said may make it a little easier, but I have no doubt it will still be difficult for you. Please, do believe it is extremely difficult for me as it increases all the more the danger of my being killed." He glanced over at Mary, aware that that would further alarm her, but he had warned her in advance that if she were to be present at the meeting, he could not mince his words with Boris—that he would have to be brutally frank.

Mary nodded reassuringly that she was okay.

Mac Ireland could see that Boris had tensed up, his back was ramrod straight, and Mac Ireland had his undivided attention.

Mac Ireland cleared his throat. "We all know what happened a short distance from here on May 13—the pope was shot."

Boris dropped his head. "Terrible, terrible, it broke my heart."

"I know, I know," replied Mac Ireland. "But here's the odd thing that I never saw coming. A priest friend of mine, who has connections with Pope John Paul II, has asked for my help. He wants to keep 'officialdom' completely out of it: the US government, the Soviet government, and the Vatican government."

"I see, I see," mused Boris with intensified interest.

"Now, Boris, my priest friend feels that because of my most unlikely background, I might be able to find out who ordered the attempted assassination of the pope… just that—who gave the order. The pope does not want to make the information public and never will. He just wants to know who wanted him dead."

Then Mac Ireland added, "As I like to say, Thomas Aquinas said that it was impossible for fallen human beings to do a completely altruistic act—an element of self-interest always creeps in.

So let me confess my little bit of self-interest: the Irish bishops have nearly always condemned the Irish freedom struggle. Cardinal O'Fiaich of Armagh is a good man. But some of the West Brit bishops have been lobbying the Vatican to get the pope to excommunicate the IRA—like Pope Pius IX excommunicated the Fenians, in both Ireland and America, on January 12, 1870. It was a shamefully political act and nothing to do with morality.

I am hoping that if I help the pope with this, it might stay his hand. It would be terrible if a pope like John Paul II were to excommunicate our Movement—and not just terrible for the IRA but also terrible for the Catholic Church in Ireland—good Catholics would just walk away by the thousands. So if it is true that the Vatican can sometimes practice Realpolitik, then I am prepared to do some of the same."

The ebullient Irish Russian was now perfectly still—not stunned or perturbed, just still, thoughtful, and totally focused.

Then Boris startled both Mary and Mac Ireland by almost shouting, "Yes, yes!"

Recovering from the outburst, Mac Ireland asked what "yes, yes" meant.

"I can help; I will do it, Patrick," Boris declared emphatically. "Yes, I can get you the answer. Needless to say, you must keep me out of it. I will do it because it is right, and I will do it in honor of Maurice Gorey, your mother's neighbor, who left the Mountain at fifteen years of age, but who never forgot Ireland or the Catholic faith.

I will also do it to honor your heroic struggle for the freedom and liberation of Ireland. I will do it, not because I am a disloyal Russian, but rather a proud Russian patriot."

There it was, what Mac Ireland thought was going to be his most difficult assignment was suddenly a walk in the park. Well God bless Kincally parish, he thought. He reached out and caught Boris's hand. "God bless you, Boris. Now please get me a one-page typed memo, of just one paragraph (untraceable, of course)—in English, Russian, and Polish. I will have it passed on to the pope, and nobody will ever know about it."

Boris briskly rose to his feet, kissed Mary on both cheeks, kissed her hand, and engulfed Mac Ireland in a Russian bear hug. "I shall be back in touch, with equity and dispatch. On that you can count, dear friends." Then he was off into the Roman night.

Good gracious, what an evening," was all Mary could manage.

"My goodness, that was unbelievable," was all Mac Ireland could muster.

CHAPTER 8

The following morning, Mary was delighted to hear that Pope John Paul II was going to make his first public appearance since the attempted assassination; he would give his blessings from the Papal Balcony at noon. She joyously shouted out the news to Mac Ireland, telling him they had to be in St. Peter's Square by at least 11:00 a.m.

By 10:30 a.m., both Mac Ireland and Mary were well ensconced in the already swelling, excited crowd in St. Peter's Square.

By noon, a massive, heaving, and voluble crowd was in place. Mary was on Mac Ireland's left, holding onto him for dear life as the crowd swayed this way and that. One guy, to Mac Ireland's right, hung on to him almost as tightly as Mary did, irritating Mac Ireland no end, but what could he do?

Then the pope spoke, and immediately the huge noisy mass of humanity fell as silent as if in church at the Consecration and Elevation, during the Mass.

"My dear brothers and sisters in Christ, thank you for your prayers. Your pope—the servant of the servants of God—is doing well. I am going to be fine. And now I bless you in the name of the Father and of the Son and of the Holy Spirit."

Then he was gone from the Papal Balcony.

The silent, bowed crowd erupted in ecstatic applause and wild cheering. The guy to Mac Ireland's right was increasing his grip on Mac Ireland's left arm, turning around so as to almost face him. The guy then brought up his right hand, and, to Mac Ireland's shock, it held, at first glance, something like a knife. It was in fact a hypodermic needle. Mac Ireland was totally hemmed in by the crowd. Mary was clinging on for dear life to his left arm, and the guy had now an amazingly strong grip on his right arm. As the hypodermic needle came up to the level of the guy's chest, Mac Ireland knew his luck had run out. All he could do was to stare and watch, as if in slow motion, his own pending execution. Then a different right hand—a very large hand—suddenly appeared, clasped the hand that held the hypodermic needle, and plunged the needle deeply into the chest of the would-be assassin.

"Patrick, no time for explanations. My great-grandfather was born across the bog from you. My name is Jeffey Mc Corry. I am in the CIA. Let's get you and Mary out of here to a safe place."

Mc Corry practically dragged Mac Ireland through the huge crowd, while Mac Ireland dragged Mary.

"What's happening, Patrick?" pleaded Mary. "Why is that man dragging you away?"

"It's okay, Mary. He just saved my life. No more questions until we are safe. Just keep up."

It took them a good fifteen minutes to exit the crowd. Mc Corry bundled them into a big SUV with pitch-black windows and ordered the driver to take off to the safe house.

Once the car was well in motion, Mc Corry turned round from the front passenger's seat and shook Mary's hand. "I'm Jeffey, Mary, and I'm here to keep you safe. Sit back, catch your breath, and we will talk once we are out of the car." He smiled and nodded reassuringly at her. She took a deep breath, closed her eyes, and leaned her head on Mac Ireland's left shoulder.

Mac Ireland was conscious the car was at times going "around in circles"—following a circuitous route to avoid being followed. He, too, had his eyes closed, wondering what the heck was going on. Fr. Murphy's words rang in his ears. "The CIA is not your enemy." It's just as well they're not, because if they were, I would now be a dead man, Mac Ireland said to himself.

In about twenty minutes, the three of them were sitting in a house in an upscale part of the city. Mc Corry had served tea and filled them in.

"The would-be assassin is a well-known—at least to those of us in the know—hit man for the Soviets. He has killed many people. One of his favorite tools is the hypodermic needle that contains a hard-to-trace deadly poison."

"Look, Jeffey," Mac Ireland responded, "I'm grateful for your saving my life, but I've real questions that I need to have answered."

"Don't worry, Patrick. The first thing you need to know about me is this: when Americans talk about 'the evil empire,' for my family, that means the British Empire.

"Obviously, the CIA has worked closely with the Brits on world affairs, but believe me, on a personal level, there are many of us who believe passionately in a free United Ireland. That goes not only for the CIA, but the FBI, the US Army, and the US police, all of which are full of Irish

Americans. You will not find one who supports the Brit-Orange position or the partition of Ireland. To all of us, that position is absurd, undemocratic, and stupid, and that is a simple fact."

Mac Ireland looked intently at Mc Corry, judging him to be about thirty-two years old. He certainly looked very Irish—sandy hair, freckled face, and fair skin. He was about six foot two, looked very fit, and was well-built with big hands. His reassuring personality clearly had put a frightened Mary at ease.

"So your great grandfather was Jeffey," said Mac Ireland. "There is a turf bank in our town-land still called after him. We grew up calling it Jeffey's bank—not, of course, a bank in which money is kept but rather a section in the peat bog from which we cut turf to burn instead of coal."

"Oh, I know, I know," assured Mc Corry. "Fr. Murphy supplied my family with a lot of photos of Jeffey's bank." He smiled knowingly and slyly.

"Aha, I knew Fr. Murphy had to be involved," declared Mac Ireland, looking reassuringly at Mary, who was visibly even more relaxed now that Fr. Murphy was in the picture.

"Yes, Fr. Murphy has been a friend of my father for forty years," Mc Corry explained. "He asked me to keep an eye on you while you are in Rome. I do not know your business here. I am just doing a favor for a wonderful priest, who has done a lifetime of priestly work for my family."

Before long, the doorbell rang, and Jeffey sprang up to answer it. He came back in a few moments and announced it was safe for Mary and Mac Ireland to go back to their house and that the driver would drop them off. Mary gave him a big hug in gratitude.

"I don't want to get involved in your business, Patrick, but you might find it easier to protect yourself if Mary was safely back in France."

Mary nodded her agreement as Mac Ireland shook Mc Corry's hand.

CHAPTER 9

Two days later, Boris Gorev called to say he had the information and he would be over shortly.

Within the hour, he was putting an envelope into Mac Ireland's hand. "As you requested, the information is in one paragraph—in English, Russian, and Polish. As we Orthodox Irish Catholics say, God be with you." Then he was gone.

Mac Ireland looked at Mary, opened the small envelope, glanced at the English paragraph, and looked at Mary again.

"There is no dilemma here for you, Boy from the Erne. I do not want to see what it says. It is best if I don't."

Mac Ireland nodded, went to the telephone, and called Fr. Murphy, who told him that Fr. Jakub Kowalski would call him shortly.

Mac Ireland made a cup of tea for Mary and himself as they waited for the call.

When Mac Ireland answered the phone, he was surprised to hear Fr. Jakub speak in a heavy Polish accent despite his forty years in America. Indeed, his accent sounded just like Pope John Paul's.

"He will see you at 11:00 a.m. tomorrow," Fr. Jakub said. "You must come alone; a car will pick you up."

"Okay, Father, but who is 'he'?"

"The pope, of course."

Mac Ireland gasped, startling Mary, who reached out and put her hand on his arm.

"Sorry, Father, can you repeat that, please? Who will I be meeting with?"

"The Holy Father, himself, the Vicar of Christ on Earth, the Pope of Rome, John Paul II," Fr. Jakub elaborated.

"Oh, my God, oh Lord," stammered Mac Ireland.

"What's the matter, Patrick? What's wrong?" asked Mary.

"Hold on, Father, please," Mac Ireland said, placing his right hand over the phone to whisper to Mary that the pope was going to meet him.

Mary put both hands to her mouth exclaiming reverently, "Mother of God."

Then Mac Ireland, pulling himself together, said, "Now, Father, if I am meeting with the pope, Mary has to come with me."

"That's not possible."

"Well, now listen, please Father, Mary has gone through a lot for this mission. She is a devoted and devout Catholic. I have to tell you—with great respect—that I am not meeting with the pope without her."

"I'll call you back within fifteen minutes," said Fr. Jakub as he hung up.

Mac Ireland looked over at Mary.

"Oh, God, Patrick, you should not have said that." Then, almost immediately, "What am I going to wear?"

Mac Ireland burst out laughing and swept her up in his arms, lifting her right off her feet. "You have put up with an awful lot, sweetheart. You deserve this."

Within fifteen minutes, as promised, Fr. Jakub was on the phone, saying, "His Holiness will be delighted to meet Mary."

Mary skipped off to the wardrobe in search of suitable attire. Mac Ireland went to find a new envelope to put Boris's information in, but he decided not to seal the envelope.

The following morning at 10:15 a.m., the car came and picked them up. By 10:45 a.m., they were seated in a private room in the papal apartments. At 11:00 a.m. on the dot, the door opened and Pope John Paul swept into the room, evaporating all the oxygen.

Though still showing signs of weakness from his shooting, the pope exuded an extraordinary aura and presence. Mac Ireland feared it might be almost too much for Mary. The pope immediately walked over and embraced her. "God bless you, Mary. I am very pleased to meet you." Then turning to Mac Ireland, the pope said, "God bless you, too, Patrick, and thank you for helping me."

Mac Ireland handed the pope the envelope.

"Please be seated, Patrick and Mary. In a moment we will have a talk, and you can tell me about blessed Ireland."

With that, the pope opened the envelope looked at it briefly, nodded thoughtfully, then put it inside the breast of his white cassock.

"Thank you, Patrick. I am very sorry about the death of Bobby Sands and the others. You know I sent an emissary to see Bobby, with my gift of a crucifix." Mac Ireland nodded. "And, I'm sure you know that I had a wonderful visit to Ireland from September 29 to October 1, 1979."

"Yes, Holy Father, but not to my part of Ireland—British-occupied Ireland."

The pope smiled broadly, obviously enjoying Mac Ireland's point. "Now tell me, Patrick, what you think of my speech in Ireland on that visit. Please speak openly and honestly. I want to know."

Mac Ireland, who had earlier wondered if the whole thing would be too much for Mary, had to admit to himself that this was almost too much for himself. Here was the intrepid Fermanagh freedom fighter, politically and militarily fearless, yet now feeling it hard to keep it all together in the presence of this gentle and nonthreatening man of God. He found himself praying for the grace to tell the truth to the pope, which in itself was so ironic that it made him smile and relax a bit.

The pope smiled at him, patiently waited, and reassuringly said, "Please, Patrick, tell me what you think of what I said in Ireland."

"Holy Father, you won't excommunicate me if I say the wrong thing?"

The pope laughed joyously. "I give you my solemn promise, Patrick."

"Well, Holy Father, with profound and reverent respect, let me say this had you said the right thing in Ireland, it's the Brits who would have shot you."

"Oh, Patrick," Mary gasped.

"It's all right, Mary," the pope assured. "I asked for Patrick to speak the truth." Mary was deeply relieved. "Please continue, Patrick."

"Well, Holy Father, in Ireland, you only appealed to 'the men of violence'—code words for the IRA—to renounce violence. You did not call on the British Government and the British Army—the fundamental source of violence—to renounce violence. You did not condemn British occupation, injustice, discrimination, torture of political prisoners, anti-Catholic bigotry, or vicious sectarianism, and all the other forms of institutionalized violence."

Mac Ireland knew he had spoken with respect, calmly and with dignity—as he had prayed he would. He looked hopefully at the pope, who was nodding his head slowly and thoughtfully, almost prayerfully.

Patrick said, "Holy Father, no country has suffered more for the Faith than Ireland. No country has shown more hostility to the Faith than England. Yet, it seems that every time the Irish rose up against oppression, the Irish bishops—with a few honorable exceptions—and the Vatican have, in effect, sided with England. The leaders of the Catholic Church have done what the great Fr. Thomas Merton warned them not to do.

"Excuse me, Patrick," the pope interjected, "you read Fr. Merton?"

"Oh, yes, Holy Father. Indeed, I always carry in my wallet one of my favorite quotes from his writings," said Mac Ireland as he pulled his wallet out.

"May I ask you to read the quote for me?"

Mac Ireland was taken aback by the pope's request, causing nervousness to flutter again. He glanced apprehensively at Mary, who nodded encouragement, and then he glanced at the pope, who graciously swept out his hand, gesturing him to continue.

Mac Ireland cleared his throat, barely being able to take in the fact that he was being asked to read to the pope. He prayed for steadiness and began reading aloud the modern day prophet. "A theology of love cannot afford to be sentimental. It cannot afford to preach edifying generalities about charity, while identifying 'peace' with mere established power and legalized violence against the oppressed. A theology of love cannot be allowed merely to serve the interest of the rich and powerful, justifying their wars, their violence and their bombs, while exhorting the poor and underprivileged to practice patience, meekness, long-suffering and to solve their problems, if at all, nonviolently."

Mac Ireland finished by saying the quote was from Merton's book *Faith and Violence*, published in 1968.

The pope nodded. "Yes, Merton, God rest him, was a great man. I'm very impressed you are familiar with him, and I thank you for reading that quote for me."

Mary beamed with pleasure and relief. Oh, thank God, she thought to herself.

"One, other thing, if I may, Holy Father," said Mac Ireland (and Mary thought, oh God, why doesn't he stop when he's ahead). "The Vatican was deeply wrong in issuing a decree of excommunication against the Fenians in Ireland and America on January 12, 1870. Pope Pius IX issued the decree. That was a terrible injustice and a great abuse of spiritual power. It, in effect, excommunicated many thousands of Irish Americans—men, women, and children—who built the Catholic Church in America. Not to mention how unfair it was to the Fenians in Ireland. The oppressed were excommunicated, and the oppressor, England, was in effect exonerated. You may not be aware of that slice of Church history, but I would humbly and respectfully ask you to take a look at it."

"Yes, yes, I will look at it, Patrick." Then the pope

paused, looked at Mary and at Patrick, and mused, "So, you think if I had called for freedom in all of Ireland, the British would have shot me?"

"I have no doubt, Holy Father. It's what evil empires do; it's the nature of the beast. For example, if there is ever war between Argentina and Britain over England's immoral occupation of the Malvinas (the Falkland Islands)—and if there were an Argentinian pope, and if he were to denounce England, watch what would happen!"

The pope sat silently, nodding his head

Then Mac Ireland said, "Holy Father, you have been most gracious. We do not wish to impose on your time. Mary and I have both our Rosary beads with us. Would you please bless them and us before we leave?"

"Yes, yes, indeed." The pope blessed the two sets of Rosary beads and blessed Mary and Mac Ireland, laying his hands on their heads. He embraced Mary, quite strongly shook Mac Ireland's hand, and said, "Go with God, in the grace of Jesus Christ, by the power of the Holy Spirit, and please pray for this Polish pope."

CHAPTER 10

Mac Ireland was delighted to receive the call from Sammy Johnson. "We will be there later on today. Those two gentlemen you encountered in France were key guys and very much involved in the cover up of the murder of my son and my aunt."

Mary told Mac Ireland she wanted to stay in, do some money managing, and be there when Sammy and Mick Duffy arrived. Liam O'Neill would be arriving by himself. That suited Mac Ireland perfectly because he wanted to go to St. Peter's and devote some real time to prayer. Still, no matter how genuinely sincere his desire for prayer, he made sure he packed his Browning HP with silencer in his waist pack. He packed twenty thirteen-round magazines in his backpack. He felt a tinge of Catholic guilt about it, but quickly and rightly squashed it with his usual exacting internal monologue. Why should the Irish soldier be the only soldier to feel guilt about fighting for justice? Why should an Irish patriot be blackmailed into feeling hypocritical if he wanted to pray while fighting for freedom? I made a vow to fight for freedom but I never vowed to stop praying. I will go and pray at St. Peter's as a humble sinner, but I cannot pretend that there are not people out to kill me. I cannot forget the guy with the hypodermic needle. There is no contradiction in that.

His inner monologue having sorted out his Catholic guilt, Mac Ireland kissed Mary, and he was off on his mini-pilgrimage to St. Peter's.

As Mac Ireland strode briskly, he marveled at the magnificence of St. Peter's Square (*Piazza San Pietro* in Italian and *Forum Sancti Petri* in Latin) 787 feet wide and 643 feet long. It was commissioned in 1655 by Pope Alexander, who made the inspired choice of selecting the great Gian Lorenzo Bernini to be the architect, designer, and sculptor.

Bernini chose an elliptical shaped square, bordered on two sides by semicircular colonnades—to symbolize the stretched arms of the church embracing the world. The colonnades have four rows of columns, sixty-six feet high and five feet wide, with 140 statues on top of the colonnades. At the center of the square is the 135-feet-high Egyptian obelisk. But that predates Bernini and Pope Alexander, having been placed there by Pope Sixtus V in 1585. The obelisk itself was transported from Egypt to Rome in AD 37.

Mac Ireland was absorbing all this like a sponge, while still keeping an eye out for hypodermic needle-bearing Soviets or gun-bearing Brits. He saw an elderly man in a familiar habit come his way. The habit was black, all the way to the ground, and around the belt (the cincture) was crisscrossed a massive Rosary—all fifteen decades. Aha, thought Mac Ireland, a Redemptorist. Those guys used to scare the hell out of me with their fire and brimstone sermons—"one mortal sin will bring you to hell for all eternity." He's not a Redemptorist priest but a lay Brother, Mac Ireland realized. As the brother got closer, Mac Ireland felt he should know him.

"Are you enjoying yourself?" asked the Brother.

"Just appreciating the vision of Pope Alexander and the genius of the great Bernini."

"Well, boyo, it was a long distance from Bernini you were born."

Mac Ireland, growing cautious but not alarmed, now felt he should definitely know this Brother. His expression was perfect Kincally. God, he thought, I hope he doesn't go into the typically Kincally ritual. Instead of introducing themselves right away like Americans do, they say, "Sure, don't you know me at all, wasn't your grandmother and me best friends?"

"Sure, don't you know me, Patrick? Wasn't I born across the river from you?"

"Oh, dear me, I can't place you at all. I'm sorry."

"I'm Brother Mick Collins. Your father and I were good friends. Your grandfather and my father were good Fenians."

"Oh, my goodness, now I recognize you! How are you?" he said as he shook the brother's hand. "How did you know who I was?"

"Because despite your nice disguise, you are still like you father."

"What are you doing in Rome, Brother Mick? I had always thought you went to the Redemptorists in England?"

"Well, I did, but about thirty years ago, the Redemptorist headquarters in Rome needed an English-speaking lay brother, so I was sent, and I've been here ever since. I have become a bit of an expert on the many different altars, chapels, and tombs in St. Peter's, and I help out here for a few hours a day. You wouldn't believe what's behind many of these famous altars, Patrick. I could hide you there from the Brits for a thousand years."

"That's good to know, Brother Mick, because I might need that." Mac Ireland laughed.

"By the way, Patrick, you mentioned Pope Alexander. See his tomb inside St. Peter's. Note where the 'Statue of Truth' has her foot placed. See you inside."

Then Brother Mick charged off with remarkable speed for a man of his age.

Once inside "the greatest church in Christendom," Mac Ireland could only feel the overwhelming power of God's Grace. The size is amazing (614 feet long, 145 feet high), but it's the Grace that matters. He headed right, to the first chapel—the Pieta of Michelangelo: 68.5 inches by 76.8 inches of awe-inspiring sculpture depicting the body of Jesus on Mary's lap after the Crucifixion.

Mac Ireland knelt in adoration: adoring Jesus, asking His Mother's intercession. How absurd, he thought, that some wrongly think Catholics adore Mary. Mary only and always points to her Son—"the Word made flesh." She, like us, was redeemed by her Son. If we take God's plan seriously, we must take Mary seriously because—under God's plan—without Mary there would be no Incarnation, no Jesus, no Death and Resurrection, no sending of the Holy Spirit, and no Redemption. As all this ran through his head and heart, Mac Ireland poured out in silent prayer his adoration of, and gratitude for, Jesus, the Most Holy Redeemer, and his traditional Kincally love for Mary, the Blessed Mother.

Mac Ireland lost all track of time. He had no idea of how long he had spent on his knees at the Pieta, but it had to be at least an hour. He decided he had to move on, visit the Blessed Sacrament Chapel, see the other chapels, and check out the monument-tomb of Pope Alexander that Brother Mick had mentioned.

He asked one of the ushers where the monument-tomb was and found it quickly in the south transept. It, too, had been created by the great Bernini. It was his final masterpiece (1678): the pope surrounded by the allegorical statues of Justice, Prudence, Charity, and Truth (which, of course, also represents Faith).

Truth, holding a symbol of the sun, has her foot placed on the globe, directly over England. That nice little touch acknowledges the pope's struggle to stop the spread of the Anglican Church and his efforts to return England to Catholicism.

Mac Ireland got a kick out of that. Fair play to you, Pope Alexander, he said to himself. It still does not make up for your predecessor, Pope Adrian IV, the only English pope, "granting" Ireland to King Henry II in 1155 through the papal decree, *Laudabiliter*.

Then Mac Ireland noticed, below Pope Alexander, that the figure of Death was represented, raising an hourglass, the artistic symbol of memento mori: "Remember you will die." At this solemn reminder, Mac Ireland bowed deeply from the waist down, in prayerful acknowledgment that he himself more than most had to be aware of death.

Immediately, three shots blasted above him, missing where his upper body had been just a split second before. Instinctively, he dove to the ground to his left and rolled over to his right, gun in hand. He spotted the would-be assassin and put him down with three shots. He kept rolling to his left, spotted another gunman, and shot him right in the chest, and then in the head as the assassin fell forward.

"Do not hesitate because you are in St. Peter's," he told himself as he got to his feet and took off at a quick run. There's got to be more of them. Judging by the way the two guys he had shot were dressed, he guessed they were KGB. He ran to the main part of the church, which surprisingly was not too crowded. Immediately, he spotted two similar looking guys staring at him intently. He buff-charged them—not really expecting to scare them—but they took off, fleeing as fast as they could right out of St. Peter's.

Mac Ireland changed direction and headed toward the main altar. To his left, he spotted three guys stalking him. Damn, now it is the Brits, from the way they looked.

As he ran around a huge pillar, Mac Ireland spotted Brother Mick Collins; he called out to him and frantically motioned him to come to the pillar. Brother Mick was there in seconds.

"I'm being hunted by two sets of assassins, Brother Mick, the SAS and the KGB."

"Bad cess to them, Patrick. The worst sets of blackguards on the face of the planet, and they have the cheek to come into St. Peter's. Fear not. Follow me."

He led Mac Ireland to a side chapel, and pulled back a red curtain, revealing a heavy door, which Brother Mick quickly unlocked. Once inside, Mac Ireland was amazed to realize he was standing in a large room that doubled as an office and sacristy.

"This is one of the places I work from. There is no way the Brits or the KGB can get in here. Let's check the surveillance cameras and see if we can spot them."

Again, Mac Ireland was amazed. When the cameras were turned on, they gave a panoramic view of St. Peter's. Almost immediately, the three Brits were visible—calmly biding their time and casually posing as regular church-going guys.

"Check the entrance," Mac Ireland said, "for the KGB." The cameras panned the entrance, and sure enough the two guys who had fled were hanging about by the doors—looking uncomfortable as if the roof were going to fall in on them.

"It's been a long time since those boys were in church," quipped Brother Mick. Mac Ireland burst out laughing, thinking it was exactly the understated type of thing his father would have said—droll and comical. "Should I have them arrested?" asked Brother Mick.

"Well, it won't do much good because their embassies will cover them with diplomatic immunity," Mac Ireland explained. "But it would give me the chance to get out of here, and, of course, arresting them would cause nice embarrassment. I'll tell you what you should do: call security and tell them to arrest the three Brits and the two KGB guys by the entrance for killing the two guys by the Pope Alexander Monument, and..."

"What's that, Patrick? Who was killed?"

"Oh, right, Brother, I didn't have a chance to tell you. I killed two KGB assassins who shot at me."

"Oh, my God," gasped Brother Mick. "But not to worry; you had to do it." He picked up the phone, told security to approach the armed suspects carefully and place them under arrest.

"Now, Patrick, let's get you out of here. Don't worry. You will be perfectly safe." He opened another door at the back of the room, which led to a maze of corridors. "Where I am taking you will lead to the left end of the St. Peter's Square (right end as you come in). I will put you in a car, and it will take you wherever you want to go. It's probably best if I don't know where you are staying, but here's my number, and you can call me if you need to. I will do whatever I can to help."

Within half an hour, Mac Ireland was opening the front door to the house. Mary ran to greet him. "Look whose here—the whole group." Johnson, O'Neill, and Duffy all rushed to shake his hand.

"Nice to see you boys. Have a seat. I have a few things to tell you."

CHAPTER 11

When Mac Ireland had a cup of tea, he called the meeting to order.

"I should tell you right away, boys, and my dear Mary, I just shot dead two KGB agents, killing them in St. Peter's."

"Jesus, Mary, and Joseph," Mary cried out and ran to hold him. "Are you okay?"

"It's okay, Mary, have a seat. Let me continue because it's urgent all of you are filled in." He briefed them, succinctly and precisely—sparing Mary's sensibilities as much as possible.

"So the SAS are here already," Johnson began. "I knew they were coming, but I did not have a chance to fill you in. Before I talk about the SAS, why the hell did the KGB try to kill you?"

"This is difficult for me, Sammy, so I hope you and the others will understand, but I cannot explain it. I gave my word I would keep a certain project confidential, but I don't think we will have to worry about the KGB again." Mac Ireland couldn't tell them that while he was with Brother Mick Collins, he had put a call into both Boris and Jeffery Mc Corry, and each of them independently confirmed the KGB-attempted assassination was a one-off—that it would not be repeated because the Kremlin did not want another international incident associated with the Vatican.

Johnson didn't hesitate a second. "If you cannot tell us, Patrick, that's okay. I'm glad we have only to worry about the SAS. And, of course, I am being totally facetious when I say 'only,' because we have lots to worry about from those boys, as you all know."

"That's for sure, that's for sure," said O'Neill. "They are one group of tough bastards."

Johnson continued: "You know, Patrick, you asked me to check on the two SAS guys you dispatched in France, and dispatched with Mary's help." Mary showed no reaction to Johnson's last comment, being still stunned by Patrick's activity in St. Peter's. "Well I checked them out; both of them were famed operators, and you were most lucky to have survived their killing skills. One of them, the bigger one with black hair, by the name of Edward Brown, was a key link in the chain of evildoers who are covering up the murders of my son Billy and my aunt Vera. Here is the extraordinary thing: I have been appointed as a detective liaison between the police and the coordinating committee, and between several military and intelligence agencies in Northern Ireland—with some outreach to the Irish Republic."

"Free State," corrected O'Neill with obvious good humor. So both Johnson and Duffy let the remark slide.

"Not only that, but the reason I was able to come to Rome is—none of you are going to believe this—they have invited me to participate in a secret conference just outside Rome, to plan how to eliminate you, Patrick, because they know you are somewhere here. They do not want to ask for help from the Italian authorities in case extradition is too messy. They want to do it the old-fashioned British way: to assassinate you. They want me involved because we are from the same parish of Kincally; therefore, they think I may have a particular insight into your Fenian head. I also suspect that—even though for the time being, they want it to be a covert action—they want it, at some stage, to be known that it was a good local Protestant that took you down, not a foreign imperialist."

"Jesus, Mary, and Joseph," Mary cried out again.

Mac Ireland took all this in stride. "Sammy, you're sure they have no idea about our association?"

"One hundred percent certain, Patrick. I know it's hard to believe, but they have no idea. I would stake my life on it."

"You are staking your life on it," interjected Duffy.

"Where is the conference, and can we execute them all?" O'Neill wanted to know.

"I have all the details, and that, Liam, is exactly what I want to propose: that we agree to kill every one of them at the secret meeting."

"Jesus, Mary, and Joseph," Mary couldn't help blurting out again. Then she said, "I don't need to know the details of your planning. Indeed, it's best if I don't. Anyway, I need to go out and check out the restaurants for our meal this evening. So excuse me now, and I will see you in a few hours." Then she headed off.

Johnson picked up where he left off. "They have rented an exclusive villa for thirteen, including me, in Frascati, which is one of the beautiful hill towns thirteen miles southeast of Rome. It is a very exclusive, and if you don't want to stick out like a sore thumb, you better rent a top-class place close by. Patrick, you told us that you would have the funds for such needs."

"For this," responded Mac Ireland, "we will spend whatever it takes—thousands, upon thousands of pounds, if necessary. This could be one of our greatest coups ever. We will spare no expense. Furthermore, we have no other great expense since we have our own supply of arms. Isn't that right, Liam? Give us a rundown on what you have in that big trunk."

"I have lots of grenades, including just stun and smoke grenades. Four assault rifles, including your AK-47, Patrick. I have three of your Browning HPs, with other handguns for all of us, and enough ammunition to fight a small war. And I have excellent bulletproof vests for all of us."

The four men continued planning for several hours.

***

Meanwhile, Mary was going in and out of restaurants with determined speed. A large American-style steak house caught her attention. It had a large deck-type veranda off the second floor, with waist-high railings, and a flight of stairs going down to a private alley, not for public use—a perfect setting for a private dinner.

She paid extra to guarantee the reservation. She paid in cash and made the reservation under the name of Windsor, which she thought was a nice touch—Windsor being the relatively lately assumed name of the British Royal Family. The Royal Family only assumed that name in 1917. Its real name of Saxe-Coburg-Gotha was changed in response to anti-German feeling in World War I. During World War I, there were seven of Queen Victoria's direct descendants on European thrones—plus two more of her Coburg relations on European thrones.

Disgustingly, the rulers of the world's three greatest nations—King George V of Great Britain, Tsar Nicholas II of Russia, and the German Kaiser Wilhelm II were not simply cousins, but first cousins. Kaiser Wilhelm II was supposed to have said that if their grandmother Queen Victoria had still been alive, she would never have allowed them to go to war with each other. Imagine how grotesque that was—that three first cousins, three spoiled brats, could officially involve the rest of the world in World War I.

Sixteen million killed and twenty million wounded in "the cousins war." Mary thought of how often she had to stop Patrick from going on about that. His reply was always the same. "If you think I'm bad, you should hear my eldest sister—who dismisses the whole bloody lot of them with 'they're all the same, they're all the same.'" Then Patrick always would complain about how the Brits got the United States involved in World War I, in effect to protect the Brits' empire in Africa and India, and, indeed, to grab new colonial territory in the Middle East. George Washington must have turned in his grave.

Of course, President Wilson was no damn good, anyway. He was a racist and a segregationist. He was an Orangeman, too. Furthermore, Woodrow Wilson made no secret about being an Orangeman. In a meeting at the White House, Mary Mac Swiney (the sister of Lord Mayor Terence Mac Swiney—the Irish hero who died on hunger strike in His Majesty's Prison, Brixton, England, in 1920) had appealed to Wilson to be concerned about British oppression in Ireland because he was Irish himself.

The old segregationist, true to form, replied, "I'm

Orange Irish." Then he went on to prove it by refusing to accept self-determination for Ireland at the Treaty of Versailles, 1919, making a mockery of his own famous words: "National aspirations must be respected; people may now be dominated and governed only by their own consent. Self-determination is not a mere phrase; it is an imperative principle of action..."

Irish Americans made him pay the price for his forked tongue by convincing, with others, the United States Senate not to confirm the Treaty of Versailles.

Of course, once England had inveigled the United States into World War I, it was easy for " the mother church," the Anglican Church, to reel in the Episcopalian Church. In 1917, Randolph Mc Kim, Episcopalian rector in Washington, obligingly declared, "It is God who has summoned us to this war. It is his war we are fighting... This conflict is indeed a crusade. The greatest in history—the holiest. It is in the profoundest and truest sense a holy war..."

And to think, Mary reflected, that John Redmond—along, of course, with Unionist leaders—encouraged two hundred thousand Irishmen to fight for England, and about thirty thousand to die.

Perfidious Albion (England) deceived them into fighting on the same side in pursuit of opposing objectives—one for Home Rule, the other against it—just as they had deceived the Arabs and Jews. The Brits even deceived their French allies, promising them that, in the spoils of victory, the French could have Palestine. That was a bald-faced lie because the Brits could not wait to get their hands on historic Palestine—the only land bridge between Africa and Asia, and (because of the Suez Canal) sea passage between the Mediterranean Sea and the Red Sea, which meant access from the Atlantic to the Indian ocean—to the Jewel in the Crown, India.

Yet, Mary continued to reflect, how some Irish—the revisionists and no-self-esteem crowd—have the gall to argue that it was Patrick Pearse who had the bloodlust, not the slaughtering empires!

That same slave-mentality crowd go on and on about Pearse's few remarks about self-sacrifice and how suffering can be redemptive, but they hardly say a word about how all three murderous empires—British, Russian, and German—did everything in their power to turn World War I into a holy war in their rhetoric and propaganda. Nor do they say a word about the empire's appalling and blasphemous attempts to identify their carnage and killing fields with the Sacrifice of Jesus Christ, Son of God, and Son of Mary. For example, in England, where the monarch is also head of the church—and where a Catholic is constitutionally forbidden to be monarch—the Anglican bishop of London, Arthur F. Winnington-Ingram wrote in 1915, "Kill Germans—do kill them; not for the sake of killing but to save the world, to kill the good as well as the bad, to kill the young as well as the old, to kill those who have shown kindness to our wounded as well as those fiends…As I have said a thousand times, I look upon it as a war for purity."

Then there is the crazed report of British General H. C. Reese (or, at least, it was a report of Reese's report by War Diary of VIII Corps, as recorded by General Hunter Weston HQ:

> I saw the lines, which advanced in such admirable order, melting away under fire. Yet not a man

> wavered, broke the ranks, or attempted to come back. I have never seen, indeed could never have imagined such a magnificent display of gallantry, discipline, and determination. The reports from the very few survivors of this marvelous advance bear out what I saw with my own eyes: that hardly a man of ours got to the German frontline.

In his lunatic bloodlust, Reese actually boasts that hardly a man got to the front line. Yes, wasn't it marvelous indeed for Jolly Old England to have suicide soldiers/bombers? You can bet they were overwhelmingly the sons of the poor, not the aristocratic rich.

That horrible little troll, Prime Minister Lloyd George, rhapsodized in Messianic terms, "The stern hand of Fate has scourged us to an elevation where we can see the great everlasting things that matter for a nation—the great peaks we had forgotten, of Duty, Honor, and Patriotism, and clad in glistening white, the great pinnacle of Sacrifice pointing like a rugged finger to Heaven."

"Does anyone ever hear the 'low-self-esteem Irish' criticize that apocalyptic nonsense?" Mary had often heard Patrick ask. "No, they reserve their criticism for our National Hero, Patrick Pearse. They are a disgrace to Ireland. They are John Bull's little toadies, and many of them are paid handsomely to do what they are doing to distract from ongoing British oppression in The North, as we speak. They deserve the contempt of every patriotic person on the island of Ireland."

Mary could repeat by heart all his pronouncements, in part, because she totally agreed with her Boy from The Erne. Furthermore, she was certain that 90 percent of the people in her own County Cavan would agree with him, too. Indeed, she felt certain that the vast majority in the twenty-six counties/Free State would agree with Patrick. It was only a small clique of would-be elites and useful idiots who parroted the old Brit rubbish that England only had Ireland's best interest at heart. It was enough to make her sick. She shook her head and said to herself, "I shouldn't give those jerks so much rent-free space in my head. Maybe, they're more to be pitied than condemned. They've turned against their own heroic little country to peddle the Big Lie of England."

***

When Mary returned to the house, she announced, "Gentlemen, although we are in Rome, I thought I would treat you all to a steak dinner. I know Liam here is a real Tyrone carnivore and doesn't want to be force-fed pasta."

"Thanks be to God," shouted O'Neill.

"Count me in on that," added Johnson. "I don't like foreign food."

"Spoken like a true Belfast man," quipped O'Neill. "Although you guys are proud to be part of a fading empire, you are, at heart, very provincial."

"Now, now, boys," interjected Duffy, "let me, being the sophisticated, urbane Dubliner, congratulate Mary on her excellent cuisine selection." Then, in the middle of laughing, he added, "Besides, I'm starving and I want some real food."

Mary ruled that the matter was settled, adding that she had selected the perfect restaurant. Mac Ireland nodded his consent, not that he had much choice.

CHAPTER 12

When Mary and the four guys arrived at the restaurant, the place was packed—the ground floor and the second floor as well.

"Look at those Italians, all excited to eat real food," joked Duffy as they walked through the noisy and loquacious diners.

Mary was delighted that their private room had been prepared with a beautiful laid out table—elegant crystals, long-stem wine glasses, and serious looking steak knives.

"Jaysus look at the size of the steak knives," marveled O'Neill.

"One could, literally, fight a bear with those," affirmed Johnson.

"So now you are going to tell us that Orangemen can fight bears," teased O'Neill.

"No, Liam, but I do know a thing or two about knifes. When we sit down, I'll tell you about it."

"Okay, gentlemen, please take your seats," directed Mary. She positioned Patrick with his back to the wall, facing the doors and the exit, knowing that's what he would want. She sat to his left, with O'Neill to his right; Johnson was on her left, and Duffy more or less at the center of the round table.

When they were seated, and the doors shut, the noise

from the larger dining room was hardly noticeable. Three formally dressed waiters came into wait on them. Only Mary ordered a glass of wine, the others just water. Mary ordered the eight-ounce filet mignon, butterflied; Mac Ireland went for the sixteen-ounce New York strip; and the three others chose the twenty-four-ounce Porterhouse steaks.

As they were munching on the great Italian bread, O'Neill said, "Well, Sammy, tell us what you know about knives?"

"I was somehow always interested in throwing knives," explained Johnson. As a boy in Fermanagh, I would practice throwing knives into trees on the farm, not that the knives were too suitable, but I got the knack of it. Then, Liam, when I joined your favorite organization, the RUC, those of us who wanted could take special training in hand-to-hand knife fighting and knife throwing. We were taught by British Army experts, and I became pretty efficient." He then paused, picked up his steak knife, and explained, "Take, for example, this knife. It is blade-heavy, that is, the blade is heavier than the handle. With throwing knives, there are three kinds: blade-heavy, handle-heavy, and balanced knives. The principle is: "Throw the weight, hold the opposite." So with this magnificent steak knife, the blade being heavier, one holds the handle to throw it. If the handle were heavier than the blade, one would hold the knife by the blade to throw it."

Then Johnson, thinking he may have gone on too long and that the topic was not the most appropriate, checked himself and said, "Well that's enough of this Jim Bowie stuff. If we are ever back on the farm together, Liam, I will give a demonstration of my Orange prowess."

Mary said, "I'm sorry you boys are not having a glass of this house red wine. It is superb." The conversation eased into all sort of chatter, stories, and jokes. The three waiters soon arrived with the steaks, and the delicious flavor and texture silenced all tongues.

While the men were still eating—and knowing no one would be ordering dessert—Mary, like they do in Ireland, slipped out of the room to pay the bill. She paid in cash and tipped generously.

When she returned, the men were still stuck into their steaks, hardly saying a word. After a short while, the doors opened again and three different waiters came in. The lead waiter held a tray in his left hand, with his right hand underneath it. As his right hand came out with a gun, Johnson yelled "SAS" and threw his steak knife with lightning speed, straight into the guy's throat.

Mac Ireland, springing to his feet—and simultaneously pushing Mary down under the table with his left hand—shouted, "Spread out, boys. Watch the stairs," as he shot the two other waiters with his silenced Browning HP: two bullets in the chest and one in the head for each. Then he sprinted over and finished off the guy that Johnson had knifed, with one bullet to the head.

Johnson took up position to the far side of the doors, Mac Ireland to the near side. O'Neill and Duffy, covering the back stairs, shot three SAS men as they charged from the stairways.

"Steady boys, there may be more," Mac Ireland directed. The doors erupted and three guys entered shooting for all their worth, everywhere and anywhere. Mac Ireland and Johnson just mowed them down, killing all three instantly.

"Are you okay, Mary?" Patrick shouted.

"I'm fine," Mary assured him.

Then three shots rang out from down the stairway, which puzzled everyone.

"Hold on," shouted Mac Ireland, and he ran over to peep down the stairs.

To his astonishment, he saw Jeffey Mc Corry at the bottom of the steps, gun at shoulder level. "Send Mary down, in case there is more shooting. We will be in the big black SUV in the alley."

"Who the hell is that," O'Neill demanded.

"I will explain it all later," Mac Ireland promised. "Right now let's get Mary down the stairs. Mary, come on, Jeffey Mc Corry is going to look after you until we get out of here."

Mary calmly walked down the stairs. The four guys huddled in the center of the room.

"Do you think there are more of them, Patrick," asked Duffy quite breathlessly.

"Well, they usually act in groups of four, even though there were only two of them in France. We have killed nine of them up here, and Jeffey has killed another three down there. So that's twelve altogether—let's wait a few minutes and see what happens.

After five minutes, they ran downstairs, into the ally, and climbed into the huge vehicle.

O'Neill quipped, "Mary, I'm glad I had paid the bill early. We wouldn't want those Italians saying we walked out without paying the bill."

They all laughed, glad of the chance to find relief in laughter from the tension of battle. The big SUV soon had them back at the house.

CHAPTER 13

When they were all safely inside the house, Mac Ireland began to introduce Mc Corry.

Johnson jumped in. "I don't care who you are. Thanks for the help."

"Oh, you guys could have handled it on your own," said Mc Corry.

"Maybe, but maybe not," said O'Neill.

In a short time, both Mac Ireland and Mc Corry had brought everyone up to speed.

Turning to Mary, Mc Corry said, "The last time I saw you, I suggested you might want to get back to France. You seemed to agree. Do you still intend to go?"

"Oh, God, yes," replied Mary. "Absolutely, positively."

"I can drive you to the airport early in the morning, and in that way ensure there will be no difficulties."

"That's perfect," Mac Ireland agreed. "Mary is much safer now away from here."

Then Mc Corry added, "Oddly enough, I think the Brits still don't know about this house. But if I were you, I would think of moving soon."

"Don't worry, we will be gone soon," assured Mac Ireland.

***

The following morning, when Mary was safely on her way to the airport for Paris, the four men got down to further planning.

"We have one week from today to plan," began Johnson. "The conference starts at 9:00 a.m. We should plan the attack for 11:00 a.m."

"Okay, we need to purchase a car," said Mac Ireland. "One that will safely get us away from the scene, but one that we can destroy. Then we have to plan to get out of Italy, and it's best if we split up.

"I guess Liam and I will travel together, and Sammy you and Mick go together. Obviously, Sammy, you are in a particularly sensitive position. You have to find an explanation as to how you were the only survivor. I am sure you have given a lot of thought to that, and you can explain it later.

"What needs to be done immediately is to find a place near the assault site, get settled in there well in advance, and we need to get a car to carry all our equipment. We have to buy it in cash, with no name attached. I think Brother Mick Collins can help us with that. He cannot be told the details. He does know that I am on the run, and he has no problem with that, so he will understand if I need to get a car without my name being attached. I can tell him to purchase it in his name, and report it stolen in a few weeks' time.

"I think he should also be the one to book the villa for us after we select it—he has the language, and he can pay in cash so that no questions will be asked. I will give him a call right now and see if he'll do it. Then we will go and, 'case the joint,' as they say in America. Is that acceptable for the moment?"

All three agreed, and Mac Ireland called Brother Mick. The good Brother readily understood why Mac Ireland would need such a car. He said a good friend of his sold used cars and he thought he could get a perfectly good and reliable car for about eight thousand pounds.

Mac Ireland told Johnson he wanted him to meet Brother Mick. "I would love to," said Johnson. "Our families have known each other for years and years." Then the intrepid four set out by taxi to case the joint in Frascati.

CHAPTER 14

In a couple of days, the four men had agreed on a safe house, albeit a villa.

It was a five-minute walk from where the Brit conference would be held. The villa was totally private, surrounded by tall walls, almost like a fortress. Best of all, from the top floor, one had a perfect view, especially with binoculars, of the conference location. With Sammy's documents, they were able to pinpoint the exact room where the twelve guys (not counting Sammy) would be seated.

A day later, they acquired a perfectly good five-seat Volvo car with a large booth/trunk; Brother Mick paid the rent for the villa and had it stocked with food, using the cash Mac Ireland provided. Johnson had the chance to meet Brother Mick, and they regaled each other with yarns and stories about their respective families.

On day four, the four men closed down their temporary headquarters and drove in their "new" car to Frascati. Another great feature of their rented villa was its enclosed parking garage, so their car could remain hidden at all times.

They had planned to go out as little as possible. However, they had made sure they would be suitably dressed to blend in—no heavy and dark clothing, lightweight shirts and pants, and sunglasses. Inside the villa, surgical gloves would be worn at all times—no exceptions. Fingerprints could not be left behind.

Once they had settled in, they felt pretty comfortable and secure, while under no allusion as to the deadly danger ahead. They were planning to eliminate twelve of the most formidable military operators on the planet: the SAS.

The SAS, or Special Air Service, was formed in 1941 by Davis Sterling. A useful distinction to remember is that British commandos specialize in attacks on conventional military targets. The SAS specializes in counterterrorism, intelligence, and reconnaissance.

Historically, the SAS has an odious record in Aden (1963–1967), Oman (1958–1959; 1970–1976), Malaya (1950–1959), and Borneo (1962–1966). They were first deployed in Northern Ireland in 1970. Working closely with the British Army's Force Research Unit—and with MI5 and MI6—the SAS specializes in assassinations, kidnapping, dirty tricks, running agents/double agents, and loyalist/Protestant death squads. In Ireland, the SAS would be seen as modern day Black and Tans—the worst of the worst. However, the IRA itself would regard the SAS as entirely formidable foes, and, in military terms, the best of the best. Indeed, some military folk would argue that the SAS were superior to the US Navy SEALs. Certainly, their selection and training are impressive. They famously train in the remote mountain range of the Brecon Beacons in South Wales. Pen y Fan is the highest point of the range: 2,906.82 feet (886 m). At the end of the first week, SAS candidates must do the Fan Dance: ascend the Pen y Fan and descend to the far side, then turn around and reverse the trek. In all, it's a march of 14.9 miles (48 km) and must be completed in four hours—while carrying a forty-pound backpack, rifle, and water bottle. The final endurance test, known as the Long Drag, is a forty-mile (65 km) hike while carrying a fifty-five-pound pack, which must be completed in twenty hours. It's all the more demanding because it comes at the end of four grueling weeks of marches and runs. Only 10 out of 125 candidates make it.

The Browning HP pistol (Mac Ireland's handgun) was the standard handgun of the SAS until recent years. While still in use, it has largely been replaced by the Sig Sauer P226.

The SAS consists of three units, one regular and two reserves—Territorial Army. The 22 SAS Regiment is the Regular Army Unit. It consists of four operational squadrons: A, B, D, and G. Each squadron has a reported sixty men, divided into four troops, commanded by a major. It is believed that each troop has about sixteen men, and each troop-patrol has four men. The Regiment is under the operational command of the director of Special Forces (DSF), who is a major general.

These were the guys Mac Ireland's team was going to take on.

***

At their first meeting in their new surroundings, Mac Ireland made the point, "Men, one of our big advantages is the element of surprise. They think they are hunting us, but now we are hunting them. Plus the fact, and it is most significant, we have a man on the inside.

"Sammy, you're the key here, but you are the most vulnerable—at least after the operation, providing that is, if any of us survives. But, of course, we are here to plan for success not failure. The last time, I mentioned that, after the operation, we had to split up—that Liam and I would travel together, and that you and Mick would travel together. Of course, I misspoke, because you, Sammy, are supposed to be a participant in the conference, so you cannot disappear, and you are going to have to have an alibi as to why you are the lone survivor.

"We need to discuss this, and we need to plan the whole logistics as to your movements during the conference. For example, are you going to be in the room when we attack? If not, how do you intend to absent yourself? Therefore, because the entire operation centers on you, I want to turn the meeting over to you because I know you have given the project a lot of thought."

"Okay, Patrick, let me give it my best shot," said Sammy. "I am still working out some ideas, and I am sure the three of you will be able to help me with that. First, I think this operation should be based on stealth and precision—not on great firepower. So I think we should not use our assault rifles. We will have them with us just in case, but do everything in our power not to use them. Furthermore, we don't want to alert the Italian authorities and police that there is a minor war taking place.

"Second, I am assuming that the twelve conference participants will not be heavily armed. Indeed, they may not be armed at all, but we must not assume that. They will, of course, have weapons in their rooms but maybe not in the conference room. Remember, too, they are Brits, and the British do not like to make a display of things. They will be going for the executive look, not the military look. They will be posing as business people or as folk on vacation.

"Remember, above all, that even without guns, these guys can be deadly, and the big danger is that if just one of them is able to get control of just one of our guns, he can kill the four of us. However, it is also true that not all twelve of them will be in top fighting condition. A few will probably be older officers, but still do not underestimate them. As you know, the motto of the SAS is this: 'Who Dares, Wins' (Qui audet adipiscitur). Our motto must be: 'Who hesitates dies, getting the others killed.' These guys are here to kill Patrick, and, therefore, all of us. We must not hesitate to kill them even if some of them or all of them are unarmed...Because if we hesitate, not one of us will make it out of that room. They will surely kill us.

"Third, tomorrow, I will check into the conference villa—as I am a registered guest, and am expected—thus I will be able to really 'case the joint.' I will get to know every inch of it and be able to thoroughly brief you.

"Four, I will leave my weapons here and not take them to the conference villa, in case the participants are searched or have to go through some screening process. If after inspecting the conference villa, I discover I can safely secure my weapons, I can make the necessary adjustments.

"Five, most importantly of all, I must figure a way to get you three into the actual conference room at exactly 11:00 a.m.—the time we agreed on. Will there be a one-door entrance, two doors, three doors? I don't know yet. We can make any of those variables work. If there are three doors, it would be ideal. Each one can make his own entrance and blast away. But you better not shoot at me."

"Especially if you have one of those bloody steak knives on you," joked O'Neill.

Johnson, broadly smiling, made a swift sweep of his hand as if throwing a knife. Then Johnson looked around the group and said that that was about all he had for the moment. The main thing he wanted the others to think about was how he could most effectively help them into the room, and what he would do when they came in, or, alternately, should he leave the room and come in shooting with the three of them.

Mac Ireland suggested that that was a good juncture to close the meeting—to sleep on it overnight and take it up in the morning.

CHAPTER 15

The following day, Johnson checked into the conference villa. The owner handed him the keys and told him the other eleven guests would be arriving that evening.

Johnson chose a lesser quality room, not just out of politeness but because it gave him easy exit and entrance to the villa. The room was away off by itself. The other rooms were on the second and third floors. The room Johnson selected was on the ground floor, as if it had been added onto the building as a separate residence for a servant or groundskeeper. It could be accessed inside the villa by a corridor leading off from the main sitting room, but it could also be accessed from the outside, having its own private door. This was a feature that Johnson liked because it gave him the opportunity to come and go as he liked—he could slip back and forth to Mac Ireland's villa unobtrusively if he were careful.

Then Johnson checked out the room that was going to serve as the conference room. It was outside, in the open courtyard, tacked onto the side of the main building, with just two small windows high up, providing no view. It had two entrance doors, which were also the only exit doors, on the same side, one to the left, and one to the right, as one faces the building. Entering the door on the left, he saw that the room was quite large. He immediately decided to set up the seating arrangements on the chance the SAS team would just go along with the arrangement as they found it.

Johnson selected four long, narrow tables, which would easily seat four persons, and arranged them in a square design, but with several feet between them. Then he placed three chairs at each table, adding an extra chair for himself at the first table to the right, as one enters the door on the left. He then removed all the other chairs and tables, neatly pushing them to the back and side of the room. He guessed there may be three senior men who would naturally gravitate to the "top table"—the one at the top left door as one enters.

It seemed an entirely plausible seating arrangement, and one that the SAS men might reasonably assume was preset by the villa owner. Of course, in reality, it was the canny Ulsterman's way of setting up easy targets—three apiece for himself, Mac Ireland, O'Neill, and Duffy.

Johnson wondered if the replacement for the late former head of the SAS Regiment would be attending the conference. Mac Ireland, O'Neill, Duffy, and Johnson had recently executed the former head, Major General Hamilton Sydney Heath, director of Special Forces, with three others—Henry George Devonworth, second in charge of MI5, British Cabinet Minister Margaret Hatcher, and the Irish politician Gerald Fitzgarret, who was also a British Agent.

Johnson felt that this time, if there were a British intelligence leader present, he would probably be from MI6 (as this was Italy, and MI6 dealt with international intelligence), rather than from MI5, which dealt with domestic intelligence. One could never be sure about this stuff.

When it suited the Brits, Belfast was "domestic," and Dublin "international," but when it didn't suit them, both cities were international. In truth, as an Ulster Protestant Unionist, Sammy Johnson knew damn well that, to the Brit establishment, Belfast was as "foreign" as County Cork. He knew most of his fellow Unionists would not publicly admit that, but deep down, they knew it. And they resented it—as all client states resent their dependence on their sponsor. Like how the new (1948) State of Israel resented its first sponsor, England, and more recently the United States—the inevitable love-hate relationship of such a setup that never works out in the end.

Johnson sat down at the "head table" and surveyed his handiwork. Not bad, he thought. He wanted to fully imbibe the feel of the room—role-play in his mind the anticipated action. He and Mac Ireland could come in the top door, shoot the guys at top table, and the guys with their backs to them—no, better one of them shoot the table facing them, because that table would have a better chance to react more quickly than that with their backs turned. O'Neill and Duffy would shoot the other two tables, three apiece. That could work. He nodded. Well in theory, at least.

How would Johnson get out of the room, to come back in with guns blazing? Should he arrange for Mac Ireland to knock, and then he would answer the door? He was much relieved to see that neither door had locks. It was a private villa after all, not a public conference location. Or should he be outside the room before 11:00 a.m. and come back in—with Mac Ireland? He would have to sort that out somehow, talk it over with Mac Ireland, O'Neill, and Duffy. However, he had already—and quite proudly—decided what his eyewitness account would be to the Italian police: he saw the perpetrators, two women and two men, flee on motorbikes, heading south. (He knew Mac Ireland and his team would be heading north toward Paris.) Both women were tall and both blond, one with long hair, the other with short hair. The two bad guys, he would explain, were at least six feet three inches, one with jet-black hair, the other almost bald and gray. Johnson would assure the Italian police that he was a trained police officer, and therefore an expert witness. Yes, he thought, with a bit of luck, this operation could go very well.

***

That evening at 9:00 p.m., England's finest arrived: masters of dirty tricks, dirty wars the world over, assassinations, and whatever was required by Her Majesty's government. They all had a grand welcome for Sammy Johnson, the only one from Northern Ireland. Johnson, like so many other policemen from Northern Ireland, always detected a bit of condescension and patronizing in their gilded greetings.

The first to introduce himself was the new head of the SAS—Director of Special Forces Major General Edward J. Brassington-Breckenridge II. A rather silly name, Johnson thought, for a very formidable man—average height, balding hair, wiry, firm grip, steady gaze, about fifty-seven years old. This guy could still kill you, Johnson noted.

The second to introduce himself was—by way of contrast—Freddy Smith, intelligence liaison. Johnson took that to mean MI6 or MI5—probably a number three or four in his agency—a bright boy, no doubt. He was about fifty years old, tall, thin, and very focused—decent sort, but not to be underestimated.

The major general called over one of the ten guys, while saying to Johnson, "Later, you can meet the others individually, but you should meet Harry now. Harry is the group leader of the nine men."

Harry casually stepped over and in a friendly manner said, "Pleased to meet you, Sammy. I am Harry Chapman. I think we can do a lot of good work together." Harry was five foot eleven, about thirty-three years old, dark hair, piercing blue eyes, broad shoulders, and big hands—a serious, cool dude. This most certainly is the man to watch, thought Johnson. This guy is capable of taking us all down. He's the first we must neutralize.

The other nine men were the real Mc Coys—serious military types, none very big, all wiry and as tough as nails. These are the boys we have to fear. Nothing will stop them but, as Mac Ireland would say, two in the chest and one in the head.

Johnson shook their hands and slapped them on the shoulder, like buddies in arms. How illogical this situation is, how dysfunctional the Northern Ireland state is, that I should have to act in this manner. As a Protestant Unionist, I should be able to see these guys as my protectors, but instead they have demonstrated themselves to be my enemies: they are responsible for the murder of my son Billy and my aunt Vera, and for the ongoing cover-up.

CHAPTER 16

As the twelve men went to settle down for the night, Johnson lay on his bed and pondered the developments that had brought him to this juncture in his life. He had come from a strong Protestant and Unionist background in County Fermanagh, just a few miles from where Mac Ireland was born and reared, in the parish of Kincally. Kincally parish was divided by The Border—the dividing line between Northern Ireland and the Free State/Irish Republic.

Johnson's entire family was from a pro-British background—British Army, RUC, B-Specials, etc. Mac Ireland was from a long line of Fenians and IRA...Yet, here they both were—in Italy, for God's sake—planning to take down the cream of the crop of the British Army... Lord, he thought, maybe prayed, this is something I never saw coming.

And, Lord, thought Johnson—and this time it was a prayer—grant eternal peace to my son Billy and my aunt Vera. Mac Ireland had convinced him that it was perfectly natural (supernatural) to pray for the dead, as most Protestants don't believe in praying for the dead. But he now found that such prayer was deeply comforting and perfectly normal.

As he lay flat on his back, Johnson recalled the devastating day he got the news his son was killed, and how strangely that had brought him and Mac Ireland together—an Orangeman and a Fenian joined in a common cause, at least to a considerable degree. It was his aunt Vera who had first brought them together. In August 1978, she had witnessed the assassin flee after killing Fr. Fergal Maguire at the altar in Kincally Catholic Church. Fr. Maguire was a close friend of Mac Ireland and had secretly performed the marriage service of Mac Ireland and Mary Mc Donough, because Mac Ireland was on the run. The priest had also revealed to Mac Ireland the identity of a top British Agent in the IRA.

When Mac Ireland discovered that Aunt Vera had seen the assassin, he went to visit her. A short time later, Vera had arranged for Johnson to secretly meet Mac Ireland in a Dublin hotel. Johnson remembered their meeting vividly, it played in his photographic mind almost like a movie. When he walked into Mac Ireland's room, he almost immediately got down to business. "Patrick, in different circumstances and maybe not too far down the road, we may end up shooting each other. I'm sure we both understand that. I am sworn to uphold the State of Northern Ireland, you are sworn to uphold a United Ireland." Mac Ireland nodded assent at that basic statement of fact.

"However," Johnson said, "I believe we can, with honor and fidelity, join forces on a particular case." He paused and looked intently at Mac Ireland, weighing him up, as he carefully chose his words. "Patrick, I have a twenty-year-old son, Billy. Well, I had—until he was murdered."

"I'm sorry to hear that. Was he in the police? Did we kill him?"

Johnson cleared his throat, took a sip of water from the small bottle on the table, and sighed deeply. "No, the IRA did not kill him. Protestant paramilitaries did—the UPF (Ulster Protection Force). They killed him because he stood up to one of their leaders who tried to bully him. I told my son always to stand up to bullies—and I taught him how to fight. Maybe I taught him too well because in a minute he had flattened the bully—knocked him out with one punch. But then my son sealed his own fate by shouting for all to hear that the UPF leader was 'a scumbag drug dealer and a murderer.' He killed the old Protestant woman down the road to cover up his drug dealing. And I have the evidence to prove it.

"A short time later, a UPF gang grabbed my son and beat him to death with iron bars. At first, I thought that was all there was to it: a revenge killing and the elimination of a possible witness. Can you fathom my horror, as a loyal Ulsterman and a faithful servant of the Crown, when I discovered that the murder was ordered by a high-ranking British counter-insurgency expert, and a key leader of the SAS in Northern Ireland? He was able to order the slaughter of my son because the UPF leader and his key associates are all British Agents and police informers, whom he has personally recruited. He is controlling them, paying them, and supplying them with weapons and information."

Johnson paused as if out of breath, the recounting of his son's slaying having taken its toll. Then, Johnson almost pleaded, "Patrick, despite the fact I'm supposed to be a hot shot detective—with all sorts of commendations—I cannot touch the killers. They are a protected species." Mac Ireland, while sympathetic, nonetheless, started to interject to ask what it had to do with him, but Johnson silenced him with an outstretched hand.

"The SAS man is the same bastard who assassinated Fr. Maguire."

"Oh, Lord," gasped Mac Ireland as he got up to pace about the room, as was his habit when he was agitated. "My God, Sammy, are you sure?"

"I am absolutely, 100-percent certain. It's my own son, after all, we are talking about." Then he almost broke, holding down his head as he whispered, "It's unbelievably painful. My heart is breaking every day. Losing Billy would be like watching my father and mother being killed before my own eyes, over and over again. It's that bad, and there's nothing I can do. That English bastard has friends in high places. Do you know what the last straw is? They took the bastard out of the North and have given him a nice, safe assignment at the British Embassy in Washington, DC."

What's his name, Sammy?'

"His name is Charlie Shepherd," he spat out.

"Sammy, what is it you want from me?"

He straightened his back, sat upright, the gloom somehow lifting off him. "I knew if I didn't give you this information, there was no way you could find out the identity of Fr. Maguire's killer—and there is absolutely no way you could discover that he had been assigned to the British Embassy in Washington."

Then it was his turn to stand up. He faced Mac Ireland and with quiet intensity declared, "I am a loyal Ulsterman, a faithful servant of Her Majesty. I would defend British interests with my life, but I owe no allegiance to murderers and to bastards who cover up murders. That is not what I am loyal to. I want to bring that bastard to justice—the final court of justice—and I think it is in your interest to help me—without either of us betraying what we are sworn to uphold. It's bloody ironic, but it's damn true. Now, Patrick, I need to say this to you. You cannot take this bastard down by yourself."

Mac Ireland bristled a little bit as he was inclined to when challenged. "Wait, now, Patrick, I am not challenging either your ability or determination, but remember, I'm a detective. I've read the massive file the Brits and the RUC have on you."

Mac Ireland winced a little bit. Johnson continued. "Patrick, don't get me wrong. I realize you are a hardy Kincally man and a fierce guerilla fighter. However, the IRA was never much trained in hand-to-hand fighting. I suspect that the only way to bring this guy down will be at close quarters and without guns."

"Don't worry, I'll fix the hoor if I get hold of him." (Except Mac Ireland pronounced it as if the word "hold" were spelled "howlt," in the way of Kincally folk.)

Sammy smiled at the expression. It brought back a lot of memories. It was just the way his father spoke. Then he put both hands on Mac Ireland's shoulders and with quiet intensity, he almost whispered, "Patrick, look at me, and listen to me. You will not be able 'to fix him.' He is the toughest bastard in the entire British Special Forces. He can kill you with his bare hands. I have been a champion boxer in the British armed services for many years—and before I joined the service, I was the champion street fighter in Protestant Belfast—and in the past, I would not have felt I could get the better of him. Now, however, because he's covered up the murder of my son, I may have the edge, and I think I can put him down with two or at least three punches. And, Patrick, you would have no chance at all in a hand-to-hand confrontation."

Mac Ireland moved back from him and sat back down on the chair. Putting his legs straight out, he crossed his ankles, showing his dark socks. "I see. So where does that leave us?"

"At the British Embassy in Washington."

"What do you mean?"

"You and I, Patrick, have to go to Washington and take the bastard down in the 'land of the free and the home of the brave.'" Then with a show of feigned slyness, he smiled. "Have you ever been to America, Patrick?" He was fully aware from his intelligence briefings that Mac Ireland had slipped in and out of America many times over the years to rally Irish Americans to the cause.

Patrick let the little dig slide. "Why do we have to go to Washington? Why don't we get him in the North?"

"I have seen the paperwork—don't ask how. He won't be back in Britain or Ireland for at least five years. They realize the only way to keep him safe is to give him diplomatic immunity and keep him in America—just like you keep some of your lads safe," he added in another mischievous dig.

This time Mac Ireland acknowledged the dig and smiled broadly. "I thought Protestants were meant to be direct—and not sly hoors," he parried. He threw his head back and laughed at the wonderful irony of it all.

Mac Ireland quickly became serious again. "Sammy, I will help on one condition. I have learned there is a British Agent at the top of the IRA—in a political position. I am not sure who it is. If you will reveal him—and I believe with your connections, you can—I will help you to take down Shepherd."

He mulled this over for a long time. "Patrick, I don't think I can. I could lose my job."

"What do you think could happen by your killing Shepherd? You could certainly lose your job for that, and I could lose my life on the streets of Washington. Anyway, Sammy, that's the way it is. If you don't give up the agent in the Movement, I will not help you, and Shepherd will remain untouchable." With that, Mac Ireland headed for the door.

"Hold on now, Patrick. Wait a second." Mac Ireland paused, turned around, and faced him. "Okay, Patrick, I'll do it if I can get the information."

"With your connections, I am certain that you can. You must get the information to me before we go to Washington. Furthermore, I will not be able to go to Washington for at least two weeks after you have given me the information."

"Fair enough, Patrick, I'll go to work on it right away."

Mac Ireland shook his hand and moved toward the door again. Just before he opened it, he turned. "Sammy, you do realize if you try to deceive me, and finger the wrong man, then the pledge I gave to your aunt, Mrs. Johnson, is voided. And I will have you killed, no matter how long it takes."

"Yes, Patrick, I realize that. You have my word. I will not play you false."

"Finally, before I go, let me mention this. Your aunt saw Shepherd leave the church. You, more than most, must understand that that puts her in real danger."

"Oh, I am acutely aware of that, Patrick. She told me

that you had advised her of the danger."

All that—in perfect recall, almost word for word, action for action, nuance for nuance—replayed itself in Sammy Johnson's mind as he drifted off to sleep, eyes moist that Mac Ireland's warning had come true. Aunt Vera was soon killed by the same murder machine.

CHAPTER 17

The following morning at a convivial breakfast, Johnson offered to show all of them around, if they wished.

"Thank you, Sammy," said the major general, "but I think it is sufficient if you just show Freddy Smith, Harry Chapman, and me the lay of the land. The other men probably want to and see the sights before our conference starts tomorrow morning. And men, all of you, that's 9:00 a.m. sharp! Then we will have a break at 10:30 a.m. and be back in our seats at 10:50 a.m. sharp so that the conference can recommence at 11:00 a.m. sharp. Now go and enjoy yourselves, and Sammy will show Freddy, Harry, and me around, and the four of us can also do some planning for the meeting." The other eight guys gladly jumped up and were off with alacrity.

Johnson very naturally assumed the unofficial role of host—a quick tour of the grand house, including a peep into Johnson's own quarters. Then the key locus: the conference room. Johnson walked in ahead of the others, made a sweep of his hand. "Hope it meets with your approval."

"Quite, quite," approved the major general, very good, indeed." Pointing to the head table, he said, "Freddy, you can sit there. I will sit in the middle, and Harry, you can sit on my right." Then, in a gentlemanly display of inclusiveness, he said, "Sammy, dear boy, where would you like to sit?"

"Well, Major General, I think I could sit here at this table on this side, by the door, so I can be the general factotum for you all."

"That's jolly nice of you, Sammy, thank you. Why don't I just jot the names down now and place them as we speak."

And on the notepad he was carrying, the major general wrote down and placed the three names for the top table, and Johnson's name on the table where Johnson was going to sit. With that, the satisfied party took their leave of the conference room.

On the way back into the villa, the major general said he was going to rest up a bit, catch up on some paper work, and that maybe he, Freddy, and Harry could meet later to go over the meeting. Sammy said he was going to go for a walk and would be back in a couple of hours.

***

The night before, as Johnson was doing his pondering and recalling, so was Mac Ireland. As is common with soldiers girding for battle, Mac Ireland reflected on his life and times, on the road not taken, and on his beloved Mary now safely in France. Also in front of his mind were the three men he was leading into battle, maybe never to return. He thought of Liam, his right arm in the IRA, and how this young man specifically came to join him—to replace Liam's own brother Kevin, who died by Mac Ireland's side. It all came back—in truth, it had never gone away—in Technicolor vividness and realism.

A couple of years ago, Mac Ireland traveled with

Kevin into Leitrim to meet with the army council of the IRA—the seven-member council that ran the organization on a day-to-day basis. The men were from Cork, Dublin, Belfast, South Armagh, Derry, and Belfast. Mac Ireland knew them all, some of them for many years.

He made his pitch quickly and to the point. "My team, Flying Column, as I still call it, is under attack. The Brits are out to destroy us. Kevin and I are here to request your total support. We can do the fighting, but we need more semtex, more guns, and more money. We need to hit back with unprecedented ferocity. Give us more SAMs, and no British helicopter will fly anywhere in South Fermanagh."

Kevin O'Neill, chipped in, fuming, "Our comrade Packie was gunned down within the Free State. The Free State makes it difficult for our men and women to move around. Yet, the SAS were able to come into County Cavan and assassinate Packie, and the useless Dublin government did not say a word."

There was a murmur of assent from the Army Council. Mac Ireland couldn't help wondering which of its seven members were working for that very Dublin government—not to mention the London government. Anyway, the Army Council pledged full logistical and materiel support.

On the way back to Cavan, and about half an hour after the meeting, Kevin O'Neill asked, "Patrick, do you think we can trust all of those boys?" When he did not answer, Kevin, who was driving, turned and looked at him, making it clear he expected an answer.

"Kevin, you are a countryman like I am. I think we have to use all our country cunning. We are in a deadly dangerous time. We have to be extremely careful."

"But, do you trust—" Before he could finish his sentence, the windshield exploded, and half of Kevin's head was blown away.

"Oh, Christ, Kevin," yelled Mac Ireland as he saw Kevin's head explode, and the car head for the ditch. He frantically grabbed the wheel and managed to steer the car so that instead of crashing head on, it scraped the side of the ditch, deeper and deeper, until it was forced to stop—still on the proper, left side, of the road.

He grabbed Kevin, but it was obvious that the stalwart young Tyrone man was already dead. He tried to figure out where the shots had come from; he heard the sound of screeching tires. He looked around and saw a car careening toward him. He then realized that the car he had seen coming toward them a few seconds earlier was where the shots had come from, and now it had reversed and was coming back to finish the job. He jumped out of the car and scrambled up on the side of the ditch. As he reached the top, two shots caught him square in the back. He pitched forward falling down through the hedge to the other side. As the car came to a halt, the shooter jumped out to follow his prey, but then a tourist bus came from behind and blew its horn loudly and persistently. At the same time two cars came from the other direction.

"Into the car," screamed the driver in his British accent. The dark-clad gunman paused, looked at the driver as if undecided what to do. "Into the fucking car, *now*!" the driver ordered.

The bus loaded with tourists, some with heads out the windows, sounded its horn again. The gunman reluctantly got back into the car, which screamed off with ferocious speed. By now the first oncoming car had stopped, and the driver had gotten out to inspect the crashed car Kevin O'Neill had been driving.

"He's dead, he's dead," the motorist screamed, and stood in front of the bus forcing it to come to a halt. "Get help, get help," the motorist screamed. Tourists rushed off the bus to gawk.

"That man has been shot," someone yelled. Pandemonium ensued.

On the other side of the ditch—unbeknownst to everyone in the excited crowd on the road—Mac Ireland's prone body began to stir. "Oh God, what's happened?" he whispered to himself. "Where am I?" Suddenly, in a flash, he knew exactly what had happened. "Thank God I was wearing my bulletproof vest." Mary had asked him to promise her that he would always wear it. He hated the bloody thing, though from now on, he would use "blessed" instead of "bloody" when thinking of it.

He peeped through the edge, saw all the commotion, and knew he had to get out of there. There was nothing he could do to help poor Kevin, and if the guards or the Special Branch caught him, there could be endless difficulties. If nothing else, he could be put away for years, or if any of the Special Branch were in the pay of the British, he would get a bullet in the back of the head. His first reaction was to keep heading on foot over the fields, but his chest was hurting and he feared some of his ribs could have been broken. He felt winded and a bit dizzy. Then he heard the bus driver shout, "Ladies and gentleman, please get back on the bus. We must be in Cavan town in one hour."

He quickly figured this was his best chance. He made

sure his wig was straight, dusted himself off, walked farther down the inside of the hedge, and exited behind the bus. The bus driver was still pleading with the tourists to get back on board. Mac Ireland smartly boarded the bus and walked halfway down where an elderly lady was sitting by herself.

"Someone has taken my seat. Is it okay for me to sit beside you, missus?" he asked politely. The lady nodded.

The bus took off. Mac Ireland closed his eyes and prayed for the soul of his trusted second-in-command, the gallant son of Tyrone, Kevin O'Neill.

All of that flashback came with incredible vividness and immediacy. But then came the pleasant recollection of Liam approaching him, wanting to take Kevin's place. It meant the world to him and, indeed, helped him to cope with Kevin's death. Many combat veterans talk about the reality of survivor's guilt: "Why did I survive, and the great man beside me was killed?"

Then Mac Ireland thought of the first time he met Mick Duffy and how that story had developed. Again, a couple of years ago, he was being driven back from Bundoran to Cavan town. Two miles before Drumshambo, he noticed a car coming up behind very rapidly. At first, he feared another ambush, but suddenly the car had flashing lights and a siren. He felt relief, which was quickly replaced by concern. Free State Special Branch—in an unmarked car—could never be a cause for rejoicing.

He told his driver to obey the siren and pull over. The Special Branch man came to the passenger side of the car, opened the door, flashed an identification card, and told Mac Ireland to step out of the car—and ordered the driver to keep going. He wasn't sure if this was just a nuisance arrest, petty harassment, or even abduction with assassination to follow. After all, just a few months ago, he, Liam O'Neill, and Sammy Johnson had executed a top Special Branch man, Brian Kelly, who was working for the British. Mac Ireland looked closely at the Special Branch man: he was in his late thirties, about five foot ten, full head of sandy hair with open, friendly features.

Smiling at him, the Special Branch man said, "Relax. I come in peace! Despite your disguise, I know who you are, Patrick." Mac Ireland was not expecting this. "Please, come with me in the car, Patrick, I want to talk to you—well away from prying eyes. Don't fret. I mean you no harm." Eying him cautiously, Mac Ireland followed him and got into the car.

"I am going to drive a few miles down the road to a quiet spot where we can talk."

The car pulled off the road onto an isolated dirt road. The Special Branch man switched off the engine, turned toward him, and held out his hand. "I'm Mick Duffy. You knew my great-aunt Lizzie Duffy in Kincally parish. My grandfather moved from Kincally many years ago and I was born in Sligo town."

He shook Duffy's hand, felt himself relaxing, but still remaining cautious. "I remember Lizzie fondly, Mick. She was a lovely woman. And (here he couldn't help but rub in it) if memory serves, she was an ardent Irish Republican."

Duffy smiled, accepting the implied rebuke.

"Okay, okay, Patrick. Don't get on your Republican high horse. I am here to help."

"Why would a Free State Special Branch man help the likes of me?"

"Because there is deep disgust and shame among some of us that one of us, Brian Kelly, was working for the British. We are glad the IRA executed him. I want to eliminate British Agents from the Special Branch—just as I am sure you want to eliminate them from the IRA."

He stared intently at Duffy, beginning to think that old Lizzie Duffy would have been quite proud of her great-nephew. Nonetheless, he declared with great seriousness, and low-keyed intensity, "Mick, if you are for real, you must realize the seriousness of what you are doing, and if you are not (and instead are trying to trick me), then I *assure* you of the seriousness of your actions."

"I am perfectly clear on both accounts, Patrick. I know I am putting both my career and life on the line."

He sat in silence, carefully weighing up his new unexpected ally. When it was clear his silence was beginning to make Duffy uneasy, he said, "Okay, Mick, what do you think you can do to help?"

"I think the number two Special Branch man, Michael Flynn—the Kerry man who really runs the Special Branch—is also a British Agent. I can prove it, but not in a court of law because the government would never allow it. If I move against him through the ordinary channels, I will be squashed like a bug and drummed out of the Special Branch in disgrace."

"How can you prove it?"

"Because when I was based for two years at the Dublin headquarters, I got suspicious of him. I followed him on a few occasions, even photographed him secretly meeting people whom I think were Brits—MI5 or SAS."

"Can I see your evidence, Mick?"

"Sure you can. I have it safely stashed away in a safety box in a bank. I can retrieve it within three days and meet with you in Dublin, a week from today."

"Let's do it. But Mick, you must now get me back to the Cavan town area. We have been here long enough. We should move before someone sees us."

"Okay, Patrick, we're off. But, by the way, what will your driver have told people about my stopping you?"

"Don't worry; he knows not to say anything to anybody until I speak to him. That's why he is my driver."

As he drifted off to sleep, Mac Ireland was very proud of Mick Duffy, and most conscious of the risks the Special Branch man had taken since that moment in the cause of a free, United Ireland.

CHAPTER 18

Instead of going for a walk as he had told the major general, Johnson, of course, slipped off to meet with Mac Ireland, O'Neill, and Duffy. The three men were relieved to see him, and were anxious to be briefed on what he had discovered about the whole situation. All four huddled around a small round kitchen table.

"We can succeed, but let me repeat the deadly nature of what we are about to do. This is one formidable group we are planning to take out," Johnson warned. However, he lightened things a bit by showing his satisfaction with the eyewitness account he planned give to the police: the four assailants, two men and two women, were on motorbikes, going south. The three men got a kick at seeing the "dour Protestant from the North" being pleased with himself.

They were delighted and amazed to hear that the major general had automatically gone along with the seating arrangement that Johnson had set up. "People tend to go along with the normal and the routine," Johnson observed. "Another good feature of the seating arrangement is that when we attack, none of us has to get close to any of the twelve targets. The room is sufficiently large to ensure that. Again, we must remember that these guys whether armed or not will still be dangerous at close quarters. So stay the well away from them. They may not be armed, but they will have pens and pencils, which are enough to kill you with—not to mention their fists, feet, and teeth. Avoid at all cost physical contact. That can sabotage the entire mission."

Mac Ireland asked, "What have you decided about where you are going to be just before 11:00 a.m. tomorrow morning?"

Johnson gave each of them sketches of the exterior of the conference room, with its two doors, high windows and the inside seating arrangements. "I think it is best for me to be in place, in the room, and just before 11:00 a.m. I will hand signal to the major general that I am slipping out the top door for a moment. I will close the door behind me, and, Patrick, you will hand me my two automatic pistols."

The three others nodded that that would work. Johnson then continued, "Then, because I have the feel of the room, I should go back in before you, Patrick. Because your entry would cause too much alarm, not to mention giving them a few split seconds warning, I will immediately shoot Harry Chapman, the Big Beast of the pack, and a man capable of killing all four of us. Next, I will shoot the major general, still a dangerous man at fifty-six years of age, and then I will kill Freddy Smith—all at the top table."

He looked around the three men to ensure they were okay with that, and then continued. "Patrick, you will be right behind me. Initially, I thought it would make sense for you to target this table." He circled with his gloved finger the first table on the right, facing inward, but I then thought that since the guys at this table would have their backs turned, it was more urgent for you to target this table." And he circled with his finger the parallel table, facing the entrance. "You see, it will take the guys with their backs turned a while longer to realize what's going on, but the guys at the table facing us will realize immediately what's happening, and we must not give them that advantage."

He looked around to make sure all three were onboard with that. They nodded. He said, "Liam and Mick, the split second you see me enter the room by the left door—as you are facing the building—you enter the right door, shooting immediately, not waiting for Patrick or me to begin. Liam, you target this table." Again he circled with his finger the table on the entrance side. "Mick you target the bottom table, facing the top table." He again circled that table with his finger to make certain there was no confusion.

"That's it in a nutshell," Johnson concluded. The entire shooting should only take seconds. The shorter the better, and the safer. Anything longer and the danger to us increases exponentially. You three then get away immediately. It will take you two minutes to run back to the house. Get into the already packed car and drive calmly but expeditiously out of Rome to France. I think Patrick and Liam should both sit in the back seat, well-down, so that the driver, Mick, is the only one visible in the car—at least for the first hundred miles or so. That helps to reduce the odds of the police pulling you over."

"That's excellent, Sammy," commended Mac Ireland. "Now, what about your own alibi? How did you survive the attack? Where were you when the attack happened? How did you see the assailants, and how did you know they were going south?

"Well, that of course that is the big question. I think the simple explanation is the best. "I went to the bathroom. I heard the shooting, and I took cover. I then saw the assailants get on their motorbikes. Taking advantage of cover, I ran after them a bit, and saw them head south." He paused, and then added, "I did a dry run, and it all adds up. It's quite credible." Then he added, "If the Italian police don't come of their own accord, in other words, if they have to depend on my calling them, I think you three will be able to have a head start of about twenty minutes or more. You see, I have to hide awhile after seeing the assailants escape on their motorbikes, in case there are more assailants. Then I have to go back into the conference room and try to help each victim. When I have verified that I cannot render assistance, and that all are dead, I have to go into the villa, find the phone, and get the police number. The Italian operator will have a problem understanding my Northern accent—so by the time the police actually arrive on the scene, you men will be long and safely gone.

"I see I'm the designated driver," said Duffy, laughing.

"Well, you told me The Guards had given you an intensive driving course," reasoned Johnson.

"And I see the Tyrone man and the Fermanagh man have been sent to the back of the bus," quipped O'Neill in good form.

"Well, like Rosa Mc Cauley-Parks, we won't accept that for too long," Mac Ireland chuckled.

Johnson remarked that he was pleased to see that all three of them were wearing surgical gloves, as he himself was—having to put them on before entering the house again. He asked if they had kept gloves on at all time since arriving at the villa.

"We have not left one fingerprint in the place." Mac Ireland emphatically assured him.

CHAPTER 19

Major General Edward J. Brassington-Breckenridge II, called the meeting to order at exactly 9:00 a.m. "Gentlemen, I know none of us like meetings. We prefer action, but sometimes meetings are a necessary evil. This is one such meeting. We have an immediate and imminent danger: Patrick Mac Ireland. The British government wants him dead or alive, but because the SAS has been given this mission, that means the Government wants him dead."

The major general paused, took a sip of water, and continued. "As always, we will conduct this meeting as soldiers not politicians." A hum of ready agreement greeted his words, with a vigorous nodding of heads. "In private, we do not try to demonize the enemy as the politicians do—throwing around insult words like terrorists, criminals, communists, Marxists, and so forth. That may make good politics but it makes bad soldiering. It can trivialize the nature and purpose of the enemy, a fatal mistake. Historically, that's what the British politicians have done in Ireland—their stereotyping of 'Paddy' made them underestimate the enemy. We know from bitter experience that Mac Ireland is no 'Paddy,' even though his first name is Patrick." He smiled at his play on words.

"Let's face it, men, deep down we all know that we

are fighting a losing war in Ireland. We know damn well that Northern Ireland is not as 'British as Finchley,' no matter how often Prime Minister Thatcher claims that. Look, for example, what is happening with the ongoing hunger strike started by the late Bobby Sands. How many people in Finchley would be prepared to fast for sixty-six days until death like Bobby Sands? How many criminals would be prepared to battle the British Army, and indeed the SAS, like the way Mac Ireland is doing? History is not on the side of England in this war."

Johnson was amazed by all this. As he carefully observed the reaction of the other listeners, he could tell they all agreed with the major general. It's a good thing Mac Ireland is not hearing this, otherwise he would find it very difficult to kill these guys, Johnson thought to himself.

"However, having said all that," the major general said, "we follow orders, we fulfill the mission, and we kill Mac Ireland and his team. Now let us seriously plan how to do that."

That rather restores the balance, Johnson wryly thought. That would've put paid to any of Mac Ireland's doubts or hesitation.

The major general then called upon Freddy Smith, intelligence liaison, to brief the group. "Both MI5 and MI6 agree that Mac Ireland operates with a very capable team. We still do not know who they are. The extraordinary thing is that no one has betrayed Mac Ireland—even though we have circulated boatloads of money. We know he runs a very tight ship, and that he knows we have agents at the top of the Irish Republican Movement—in Sinn Fein and the IRA. Indeed, Mac Ireland has executed a number of such agents.

"We know he has no political ambition. He is just interested in the cause—that is, ending England's interference in, and sovereignty over, Irish affairs. He is very Catholic, but also very nonsectarian believing that sectarianism is the antithesis of Catholicism. He likes to quote the famous expert on world religions, Mircea Eliade, who states that the opposite of Catholicism (which means universal/whole) is not Protestantism but sectarianism. We also know that he is totally loyal to his Movement, and if a settlement is reached, he will honor that and never cause a split. He abhors splits. In other words, he is the perfect man for his job. We must be perfect men for our job. And our job—as the CIA says—is to exterminate him with extreme prejudice."

Harry Chapman, the group leader, the Big Beast, was the next to speak. "Men, I agree with what has been said. Mac Ireland is a fine soldier and probably, in his own way, has respect for the SAS. However, we are preparing to be in full operational mode, and as such, we have to kill the bastard. I want to put a bullet, no several bullets, in his Irish Catholic head. We have him on the run. We must finish the job. My latest information is that our last attempt at the restaurant in Rome spooked him badly, and he's probably left Rome by now or is in deep hiding. We will track him down, and shoot him like a dog. He has killed a number of my good friends. He has embarrassed and humiliated the SAS, and we have to exterminate the bastard, by any means necessary."

Johnson watched all this in fascination: almost the good cop–bad cop variation.

The other two speakers had oozed objectivity and common sense, but the job of the Big Beast was to gird his men for battle. No more nice and casual Harry. This Harry was now a ferocious warrior, and a most deadly one. But making it all the more easy for me to have to kill him, thought Johnson.

"From this moment on, men," Chapman ordered, "our top priority is to kill Mac Ireland and his team. He's on the run. He's the prey; we are the hunters. Whether we get him in Europe or Ireland, we shall get him. However, we do have to be extra careful not to cause an international incident while in Europe, because you know the politicians will hang us out to dry. We can do what we like in Britain and Ireland, but here in Europe, there are restrictions. However, we must not let that interfere with our getting Mac Ireland. If we see our chance, we take it—and damn the consequences." Certainly no more nice guy, affirmed Johnson to himself.

The meeting was then opened up for general discussion, which drifted back and forth. At 10:30 a.m., the major general announced the real logistical planning would not begin until after the recess, and firmly reminded them they had to be back in their seats at 10:50 a.m. for the meeting to recommence at 11:00 a.m.

CHAPTER 20

The major general sure does run a tight ship, Johnson thought to himself as the seats filled at 10:50 a.m. In ten minutes, it will all begin, he said to himself, surprised at his own calmness and focus.

At 11:00 a.m.—D-day in Johnson's mind—the major general rapped the meeting back to order and began to give instructions. Johnson indicated with his hand that he was slipping out; the major general nodded his understanding and continued talking. Johnson closed the door behind him. To his left by the door, Mac Ireland was poised for action, and O'Neill and Duffy were poised by the other door. Johnson slipped on his surgical gloves as Mac Ireland gave him his two guns.

Mac Ireland whispered, "One, two, three, go." Johnson, in first, blasted the top table—killing Chapman before he could get out of his seat, and killing the major general and Freddy Smith, who never even tried to get out of their seats.

Simultaneously, Mac Ireland blasted the three men facing him at the table across the room. One of them got off a shot, hitting Mac Ireland straight in the chest, stumbling him back with the blast. The guy Jonson had been sitting next to, and who had just been shot in the back by O'Neill, somehow incredibly pounced on top of Mac

Ireland, furiously stabbing him with a pen. When he realized Mac Ireland's bulletproof vest was absorbing the blows, he went for Mac Ireland's eyes. Mac Ireland covered his eyes with his forearm as the pen ploughed into his flesh. Then the SAS man went for the throat, but before the blow could land, Johnson placed his foot over Mac Ireland's throat, diverting the blow. Simultaneously, Johnson grabbed the hair of the attacker, jerked his head back, put his gun to the guy's ear, and practically blew his head off. Meanwhile, O'Neill and Duffy had finished their jobs.

Johnson helped Mac Ireland to his feet. As Mac Ireland caught his breath, he said, "Sammy and Mick, if you leave any witnesses, your cover will be blown. Finish them off and make sure everyone is dead."

The two policemen—one an RUC man and the other a Dublin Special Branch man—calmly fired a shot into the heads of the twelve, probably already dead, men.

Johnson handed his guns and his surgical gloves to Mac Ireland, saying, "Go men, calmly but quickly, and good luck."

Surveying the carnage, O'Neill said, "That is partial payment for the SAS murder of my brother Kevin."

Mac Ireland added somberly, "And partial payment for Bobby Sands and his fellow martyrs. The names of these twelve Brits will never be remembered, but the names of Bobby Sands and his companions will live forever in Irish history."

On that note, Mac Ireland, O'Neill, and Duffy vanished.

CHAPTER 21

Duffy, cool as a cucumber, drove for four hours away from Rome. Then O'Neill took over for another four hours. Then Mac Ireland for three hours, the stab wounds in his left forearm no longer of any concern. While Duffy was at the wheel, O'Neill had cleansed Mac Ireland's wounds and bound them sufficiently.

After eleven hours of shared driving, the three were safely in a little hotel in Lyon, France. Mac Ireland called Mary at her friends' house. "Mary, all is well. We will see you in Paris tomorrow. Please arrange for your friends to fly Kevin, Mick, you, and me to Ireland in their private plane in a few days. Sammy is making his own arrangements."

Mary was anxious to talk, but Patrick advised it was best to wait until they met. Once Mary knew they were all safe, she was happy enough to wait.

"Good night, sweetheart. The Cause endures," Mac Ireland assured.

48842128R00076

Made in the USA
Charleston, SC
13 November 2015